# LUCY DANIELS

# Gorilla

## — *in the* —

# Glade

*Illustrations by Ann Baum*

*Hodder
Children's
Books*

a division of Hodder Headline plc

*To Celia Jane*

**Special thanks to Ingrid Hoare.**

**Thanks also C. J. Hall, B.Vet.Med., M.R.C.V.S., for reviewing the veterinary information contained in this book.**

Animal Ark is a trademark of Ben M. Baglio

Text copyright © 1999 Ben M. Baglio
Created by Ben M. Baglio, London W12 7QY
Illustrations copyright © 1999 Ann Baum

First published in Great Britain in 1999
by Hodder Children's Books

The right of Lucy Daniels to be identified as the author of this work
has been asserted by her in accordance with the Copyright, Designs
and Patents Act 1988.

10 9 8 7 6 5 4 3 2 1

A Catalogue record for this book is available from the British Library

ISBN 0 340 73594 5

Typeset by Avon Dataset Ltd, Bidford-on-Avon, Warks

Printed and bound in Great Britain by Clays Ltd, St Ives plc

Hodder Children's Books
a division of Hodder Headline plc
338 Euston Road
London NW1 3BH

# GORILLA IN THE GLADE

John Carter saw Mandy's unhappy expression. 'No baby gorilla could have had better care than Jojo has had,' he said kindly. 'But gorillas are highly intelligent animals and family life is very important to them. My guess is that he's pining for a life that he senses is out there in the forest somewhere . . . Jojo wants to be with his own species.'

'So, what can we do?' Mandy asked anxiously.

'Well, we've got to do our utmost to find Jojo a gorilla mother as soon as possible,' Mr Carter went on.

'Grace,' said Mandy softly. 'She's our only hope.'

Mr Carter nodded. 'But Mandy,' he warned gently, 'Grace might decide she doesn't want Jojo, like his natural mother did.'

Mandy's face fell. She couldn't bear the thought of that. *Oh, Grace*, she pleaded silently, *please don't let us down. Jojo needs you!*

*Animal Ark series*

# *One*

'The water's scorching!' yelled James Hunter from inside the small wooden hut that served their African camp as a shower. 'And there's not even a hot tap!'

From where she sat under a nearby frangipani tree, Mandy Hope laughed gleefully at her best friend. 'Of course it's hot, James! This is Africa, remember!' she called to him.

The canvas curtain to the stall was taking a buffeting as Mandy's friend danced about to avoid the cascade of scalding water. The shower was fed from an oil drum set high in the branches of an overhanging tree. Its metal sides had been baking in the African sun since dawn and now it was late afternoon.

'James performing a rain dance in that hut?' asked Mandy's father, Adam Hope, coming over to offer her a glass of lemonade.

'He was hot, so he thought he'd shower. Now he's even hotter!' Mandy told him. 'Thanks, Dad.' She took the glass gratefully. She was so parched she could have drunk a lagoon. 'I'm going to wait for the sun to go down before I attempt a shower!'

'Good idea,' said Mr Hope, peering up curiously at the suspended oil drum from under the brim of his peaked cap.

The lemonade was flat, but refreshing. Mandy noticed that the force of the afternoon heat was fading and the sky was turning a light, milky-orange colour. It looked beautiful; so different from an English sky. She thought of her home in Welford, so many thousands of miles away in cool, ordered Yorkshire. It had been sad to say goodbye to Animal Ark, and to Gran and Grandad Hope . . .

But the excitement Mandy felt at being back in Africa, where she'd had marvellous adventures, had started on the drive to the airport – and it was with her still. It was hard to believe she was here at Camp Kahuzi – in the middle of the vast, lowland rainforests of Central Africa.

Mandy looked out into the dim shadows surrounding the camp. The forest floor gave off a hot and musty smell. Mandy could imagine the many creatures going busily about their business in its steaming depths . . .

Camp Kahuzi was a small workstation and base within the protected boundaries of the huge Kahuzi National Park. It had been set up for the scientists and conservationists who came to study the local gorilla population. Mandy couldn't believe how lucky she was.

But already their holiday here was racing past. Mandy looked at her wristwatch. They had been in Africa for almost one whole day! There was not a minute to be lost. She jumped up, pushing back the strands of blonde hair plastered stickily across her damp forehead, and set off to find her mother and Levina.

Barefoot, Mandy trod carefully and crossed the prickly grass clearing to the muddy pink structure – a cross between a cheerfully painted corrugated iron shack and a luxury tent –

that served as both camp canteen and office. Slipping in under the mesh of the fly-screen, she found her mother and Levina peering at a map that was spread out across a table piled high with papers. A small typewriter and a two-way radio took up most of the available space on the desktop.

'Seen anything interesting yet?' Emily Hope looked up from the map and smiled at Mandy. She had twisted up her long auburn hair into a bun on the top of her head to try to keep her neck cool.

'Only James, trying to manage the shower!' laughed Mandy. 'Will any animals come wandering right into camp, Levina?' she asked.

'Occasionally. We get a few creatures whose curiosity gets the better of them from time to time . . . small monkeys, the odd snake . . .'

'Great!' said Mandy. 'And . . . when will we go out into the forest to look for gorillas?' she asked.

'Whoa!' chuckled Adam Hope, ducking in under the fly-screen, holding a tin tray. 'We've only just arrived, Mandy. Give us a chance to unpack before we dash off again!'

'Sorry, Dad,' sighed Mandy, handing her

mother and Levina a glass each from the tray. It was hard to curb her impatience to explore the wonderful places she travelled to with her parents. Mrs Hope had just spent a few months working in China, and then India. Mandy, James and Mr Hope had joined her for holidays, and now Mrs Hope had stopped off on her journey home to join them in Africa for a holiday with Levina.

Like Mandy's parents, Doctor Levina Lemiso was a vet. Emily and Adam Hope had made friends with her during their time at veterinary college in York. Born in Tanzania in East Africa, Levina had studied in England, then returned to her homeland to work as a research scientist. Now she had invited the Hopes to visit her in the Democratic Republic of the Congo, in Central Africa, where she was based while she prepared a television documentary about gorillas.

'We have another guest arriving tomorrow,' Levina said. 'So perhaps not until the afternoon or the day after. Actually, your mother and I were just plotting our route through the forest.'

'Oh, *great*! said Mandy again. 'I'll go and tell James.' She raced out of the door.

Mandy found James wrestling with a large tent. They were one sleeping-hut short in the camp, and James had volunteered to sleep outdoors. The tent was khaki-coloured, dome-shaped and flapped about in the evening breeze like a large bird caught in a trap.

'Nice shower?' Mandy asked him, picking up a mallet to help him hammer a tent peg into the earth.

'Very funny,' retorted James, grimacing. 'What's your hut like?'

'Fine,' Mandy replied. 'Circular, and just big enough for a camp-bed. The floor is earth, but it has a nice rug on it. And it has tons of spiders living up in the pointed grass roof!'

James wrinkled his nose.

'Levina says we're going to go off exploring the day after tomorrow, to see if we can find the gorillas,' Mandy told him.

'Oh, wow!' said James, his eyes shining. 'Is the television camera bloke coming along, too?'

'Paul Wilkie? I expect so. Levina says he's gone off into the forest, but he's coming back to the camp for supper this evening. We'll ask him then.'

When the last peg had secured the tent to

the earth, James went off in search of a ground sheet and sleeping bag.

Mandy lifted the tent flap and crawled in. The setting sun burned fiercely on the fabric sides of the tent, turning the light on the inside a hazy coppery colour that Mandy loved.

She began to flatten the earth with the palms of her hands, smoothing it and separating out the little stones to make it more comfortable for the night ahead.

On her hands and knees, absorbed in her task, Mandy became aware of a strange grunting sound. She stopped to listen. A snorting, scuffing and snuffling sound . . . growing closer, louder. 'James?' she said. 'Is that you out there?'

A squat, shadowy shape loomed up against the side of the tent, and leaned heavily against it. Mandy could hear the rasp of breath and a soft squealing. For an instant, she was absolutely frozen to the spot, then she decided to retreat. But before she could move, the base of the tent was nosed up off the ground and she came face to face with the ugliest creature she had ever seen!

Mandy had seen warthogs before, but she had never been face to face with one. The hog's

little piggy eyes peered at her in alarm. His bristly black snout quivered as he drew in her scent, working his stumpy yellow tusks up and down and tossing his head.

Mandy kept very still. The blood was pounding in her ears. And then the warthog wheeled around, kicked up his back legs and ran off at top speed back into the depths of the forest.

The tent, uprooted from its moorings, collapsed with a sigh around her. Mandy was so relieved she began to chuckle. It took a few minutes before she felt able to slide her way over to the tent's opening and try to squeeze out. She poked out her head, the tent hanging like a headscarf over her ears.

James was striding across towards her, a sleeping bag in his arms. He stopped dead when he spotted her and wrinkled his freckled nose. 'Honestly! I leave you alone for five minutes and just look what you've done to my tent!'

'It was just about the biggest fright, ever!' Mandy finished. She'd been telling the story for a second time for the benefit of Paul Wilkie, the cameraman, who had arrived late for a fireside supper. They were all enjoying a second helping of boiled chicken and vegetables, served up by Manou, the camp cook.

Mandy had explained to Manou that she was a vegetarian, and so he had given her an extra big helping of the vegetables and some delicious bread that he'd baked that day.

'I'd like to bet that poor warthog is still running!' Paul laughed a deep, rumbling laugh. 'I'm sure he got an even bigger fright than you did, Mandy.'

Mandy smiled at him. James was looking at Paul too, trying not to stare. But it was hard not to. Paul Wilkie was quite striking. An enormous man, he towered over Mr Hope, and his long fair hair was tied back in a ponytail. He had trained as a zoologist and now worked as a wildlife cameraman. His job had taken him all over the world, filming animals in many faraway and exotic locations.

'I wish I had thought to warn you about that little fellow,' smiled Levina. 'He's been seen in the camp a few times. Seems very curious about our comings and goings. We've nicknamed him Rumba, after the way he wiggles his backside.'

Everyone laughed. The sky was an inky blue and the first bats were swooping and diving, making little jinking noises above their heads while below, from the ground, came the cheerful chorus of crickets. Huge moths had gathered around the glass shades of the oil lamps that burned on the table.

'Will you be going with us into the forest?' James asked Paul.

Paul nodded. 'I'm looking forward to getting something on film,' he replied.

'Our aim is to watch and record the social habits of a family group of gorillas,' Levina explained. 'The band of gorillas we've been following in the last few weeks are getting used to us being around now, and don't seem to mind too much.' She waved away a mosquito. 'But tomorrow,' she added, 'John Carter is arriving.'

'John Carter . . .' Mandy echoed. 'I've heard that name before . . .'

Levina smiled. 'Quite likely. He's the owner of a zoo in the south of England that is dedicated to breeding animals in captivity to release into the wild. He's particularly fond of gorillas, and is an old friend of Camp Kahuzi. He makes regular trips to check on how the animals that he has brought here are getting along.'

'Can't the gorillas be left to breed by themselves, right here?' Mandy asked.

Levina shook her head. 'Gorillas *are* breeding by themselves, here in the Congo, and in other parts of Africa,' she explained, 'but not in numbers that will keep the species safe from extinction.'

'Why is that?' James asked.

'A number of reasons,' Levina told him. 'Their forest habitat is being cut back to make way for people, and they are trapped by hunters – for illegal trade and for food. Gorillas are often taken from their mothers in the forest when they are very young—' Levina broke off.

Mandy could see by her face how upsetting it was for Levina to talk about this. Mandy was feeling upset herself at the thought of a baby gorilla being deliberately separated from its mother.

She felt a comforting hand on her arm. 'But reserves like Camp Kahuzi help to protect the gorillas,' Emily Hope said gently.

Mandy nodded and forced a smile.

'So this man . . . Mr Carter,' James asked, 'does he bring the gorillas back to the forests and just let them go?'

Levina shook her head. 'John brings the gorillas back to the reserves, James,' she explained. 'He releases them here where they will be protected and left in peace to thrive.'

'And peace is just what I need right now,' said Mr Hope, stretching his hands out to the fire and yawning. 'I'm ready for my camp-bed. Anyone else?'

'Yes,' James agreed. He stood up and looked across at his tent, now upright again. 'Just one thing . . . am I likely to have a second visit from Rumba tonight, d'you think?'

There was a rumble of laughter from Manou. 'Not tonight,' he said. 'I put plenty garlic in food. Rumba, he don't like the smelly garlic!'

# *Two*

Mandy was woken by the sound of the camp Land-rover revving its engine. For a moment, she couldn't think where she was. Then she breathed deeply and smelled the scents of a new day. Damp earth after a night of dew; the bougainvillea blossoms climbing outside the window of her hut; the wonderful aroma of frying eggs and tomatoes.

She leaped off her bed and looked out. The cluster of little huts within the circle of dense forest was bathed in a soft morning mist. It was magical.

Camp Kahuzi! The gorillas! She might well

see the wild apes in their own habitat later on.

Mandy snatched up a pair of shorts and a T-shirt. Then she remembered she had forgotten to have a shower the previous evening. She dismissed this as being too unimportant to worry about and dashed out.

Manou was crooning a song in his own language as he stood over a large sizzling pan.

Mandy called out to him and waved. She spotted James over by the Land-rover, helping to load some cardboard boxes and other equipment.

'Thought you'd never wake up,' he said, as Mandy came over. 'Some of us have already had breakfast!'

'I took ages getting off to sleep,' Mandy replied. 'I wish we hadn't had that conversation about the poor gorillas just before bed.'

'Me too. That – and the thought that Rumba might come visiting – kept me awake, I can tell you.' James shifted his glasses higher up on his nose. Though it was only eight in the morning, he was perspiring, and his glasses would insist on sliding down the bridge of his nose at every turn.

'Paul is going to the post office and taking

some bits and pieces to the research offices. I'm giving him a hand to load up,' James continued. He pointed over to the camp truck. 'And Kadebe – that's the man under the bonnet – is driving to the aerodrome to pick up Mr Carter soon. He asked if we wanted to go along for the ride.'

'No, you go,' Mandy said. 'I'll stay in camp. I don't want to miss out on that breakfast – my mouth is watering!'

'I think you might find I left you a few scraps, but only a few,' James grinned.

Mandy walked over to join her parents and Levina at a table spread with a fuchsia-pink cloth.

Mandy recognised the *mielie* meal, a kind of sticky white porridge that she had enjoyed during her last visit to Africa. She followed this with some of the piping-hot fried eggs and tomatoes, and chunks of bread torn from the crisp, round loaves Manou had just baked.

Mandy was still sitting at the table, too full to move, when she heard the sound of the truck returning with John Carter.

Levina and the Hopes stood in a group to

welcome their important visitor into the camp. As the truck pulled to a slow halt in front of them, the passenger door opened.

A rather stern-looking man in his late fifties climbed out stiffly. 'I'll never get used to the bumps in African roads!' he groaned. Then he smiled, blue eyes twinkling under the brim of his straw hat, and held out his hand to Levina.

'Delighted to meet you, at last!' she said, smiling back.

John Carter had a bushy white beard that reminded Mandy of Father Christmas. Still smiling, he greeted each of them in turn.

Mandy noticed that James had jumped down from the truck and was peering into the back. He looked as though he was about to burst with excitement.

'Ah, yes,' said John Carter, scratching his beard. 'I must introduce you to my young charge there.' He turned to James. 'Give me a hand, will you, lad?'

James sprang into the back of the truck and carefully heaved out a wooden crate. It had several large holes all over the sides and top. From one of the holes, a small black hand was poking out; tiny leathery fingers waved comically at nothing in particular.

Mandy's eyes opened wide with excitement. 'Oh!' she said. 'Look! Mum, Dad, look!'

Mr Carter was undoing the clips that held the lid of the box secure. 'Hello, young man,' he said, and lifted up a tiny gorilla, wrapped up like a parcel in a large white nappy.

Holding the baby animal in his arms and stroking its back, Mr Carter turned to the others, saying, 'This is Jojo. He's an orphan and in need of a bit of love and attention.'

Jojo wound his long arms round Mr Carter's neck. Safe with the man he knew and trusted, he slowly blinked his eyes against the glare of the sun and stared curiously around at the new faces looking back at him.

Mandy's heart clenched. The tiny gorilla looked so sad, she thought – and so human that she almost expected two large teardrops to squeeze from his big, brown eyes and slide down his furry face. 'Did his mother die?' she whispered, frowning up at Mr Carter.

'No. Just didn't want to be a mother,' he replied, matter-of-factly. 'Wouldn't have anything to do with the little chap after he was born. We left him with her as long as we could

– a day and a half – but he started to weaken. She wouldn't feed him, you see,' Mr Carter explained. 'So we had to get him used to taking a bottle.'

'How old is he?' Adam Hope asked, smiling at the enchanting little ape.

'Coming on for . . . ah, about four and a half months now,' Mr Carter replied.

Mandy put out a tentative hand to Jojo and he quickly buried his face in Mr Carter's neck, like a shy toddler.

John Carter saw the look of disappointment on Mandy's face. 'Tell you what,' he said, 'Jojo is going to need lots of care until we can find him a new mum. 'I'm going to be very busy checking up on the gorillas in the forest and catching up on some important paperwork. Can I rely on you and James to look after him?' he asked, looking at both of them.

Mandy looked over at James, unable to believe their luck. He was beaming and nodding his head. 'Oh, yes, please,' she said. 'We'd like that. James and I will make a great gorilla-sitting team!'

'Good,' said Mr Carter, satisfied. 'Now, come on you lot, Jojo and I need a long, cold drink.'

Kadebe carried John Carter's luggage into the camp area, and over to the small circular *rondavel*, or hut, that had been reserved for Mr Carter's use.

'Aha!' laughed Mr Carter. 'The luxury suite!'

Manou was hurrying over to the hut with a large bucket of hot water and a towel over his arm, like a butler at a smart hotel. '*Habari Mzungu?*' he greeted, in his language.

'*Mazuri sana*, Manou,' John Carter replied, bowing his head respectfully.

Mandy thought she was going to like John Carter very much and was glad that he had joined them. Now, there was the added bonus of a baby gorilla to care for too. She caught James's eye and grinned. It was going to be a wonderful holiday.

In a small wooden outbuilding, no longer used as an office, Mandy and James began to set up a 'nursery' for Jojo. They had left him with Levina, who was encouraging him to try a piece of soft fruit. Paul Wilkie was taking photographs of them.

Mandy hadn't yet had a chance to hold Jojo and she couldn't wait to cuddle his hairy little body against her. She had asked John Carter if he thought Jojo was suffering because his mother had rejected him.

'It's difficult to know, Mandy,' Mr Carter had replied, tugging thoughtfully at his beard. 'But as long as he gets a lot of affection and care from somewhere, I expect he will thrive.'

Mandy had determined there and then to give Jojo all the love and care he needed.

First, she and James borrowed a broom – a bunch of dried grasses tied with a leather thong – and brushed out the dusty floor of the hut. Geckos, small and large, scattered up the walls in fright.

'Ugh! Spiders,' James said. Their darting, hairy bodies scrambled for cover wherever they could find it.

'Well . . . not for long,' Mandy replied bravely, and swept those that she could reach gently out of the door.

Levina had supplied them with a few old cushions and Kadebe had donated some strong, brown cloth sacks, once used to transport maize meal to the camp. In one corner of the room they made up a bed for Jojo, and in the other they heaped a pile of grass, leaves and twigs.

Paul Wilkie put his head in around the door and smiled at the work going on inside. He had taken off his T-shirt to soak up the sun and his skin was already as brown as mud. 'I'll go into the forest and fetch some vegetation for the little guy,' he volunteered. 'Just to remind him . . . ah, that he's an ape, you know?'

Mandy grinned. 'He's only a baby, for the moment. But, yes, please. That would be great.'

Paul returned with a mini-jungle in his arms; whole branches to cling and climb on, some of them sporting a mass of greenery, turning Jojo's haven into a magnificent playpen as well.

'Goodness!' exclaimed Mandy. 'We'll lose him in all that!'

'It's for privacy,' Paul explained. 'To give him a place to hide when he wants to.'

Finally, Mandy stood back to admire their handiwork. She and James were satisfied that Jojo would love this little room. There was only one thing missing.

'Toys!' Mandy said. 'We haven't any toys for him to play with.' They went off in search of a solution to the problem.

Levina came up with a brightly coloured necklace of large beads strung on a strip of leather. When she danced it about, it made a rattling sound. 'He's too little to try and swallow them, just yet,' she smiled. 'They might amuse him.'

Manou donated a wooden spoon and an old plastic mixing bowl to the cause. Mandy was delighted.

All during their lunch of tinned fish and salad, Jojo slept soundly in John Carter's lap. Mandy could hardly eat for looking at him. Jojo's hands and feet and face were tucked up so neatly that, from a distance, Mandy thought it looked as though Mr Carter had simply removed a rather hairy black jumper and put it on his knees.

'It's a shame Jojo didn't have a twin sister or brother,' James said.

'Female gorillas can usually only have one infant at a time,' John Carter explained. 'And they only do that every four years. Like human babies, gorilla babies need a lot of careful love and attention in order to survive.'

Mandy and James listened, fascinated, as John Carter went on. 'Infant gorillas are completely dependent on their mothers for food and protection at first. They drink only their mother's milk until they are about two and a half months old. Then they start to crawl around, and will take a little vegetable matter. But they will continue to go to their mother for milk until they are nearly two years old. And live for about forty years, if all goes well . . .'

'When will Jojo be able to walk?' James asked.

'At about eight months,' Mr Carter replied. He turned Jojo round in his lap, and the gorilla stretched his little body as he slowly awakened. 'Would you like to try giving him a feed now?' he asked.

Mandy and James nodded eagerly and went over to the kitchen, where Manou was carefully following Mr Carter's instructions and heaping milk powder from a large tin into a baby's bottle. He frowned with concentration as he poured the cooled, boiled water into the bottle, screwed on the teat and shook the mixture vigorously.

Manou handed the bottle to Mandy and smiled a dazzlingly white smile. 'Now, ape baby he drink milk. But later,' he confided, 'ape baby like to eat cockroaches, grasshoppers, millipedes and palm-maggots. You must catch them for him, yes?' Manou roared with laughter at the thought of Mandy stalking through the jungle in search of gorilla food.

A few seconds later, Mandy sat with Jojo under the shade of a large, vine-covered tree. His shiny eyes were fixed on the bottle in Mandy's hand and he stretched out an arm in eagerness. Then he settled happily up against her, lying back like a human baby, his long, black fingers and his toes gripping the bottle all at once. He sucked noisily while Mandy and James watched him, fascinated.

When he had finished his bottle, Jojo looked up and fixed his big dark eyes on Mandy. With a finger she wiped the milk-tide from round his

black lips, then gently put her nose against his and rubbed. Jojo's tiny black nose was warm and dry, and he smelled like a baby; milky-sweet. Mandy stroked his flat little ears and smiled at him.

Jojo seemed to relax. His body flopped and he put out a tentative finger to mimic Mandy, touching her ear. Then he lifted his top lip and showed her his pink, toothless gums.

'He's smiling,' said James, in wonder. 'It's going to be all right, Mandy.'

When Levina came over with Adam and Emily Hope, they found Mandy and James in fits of giggles. Jojo, his tummy full of warm milk, was showing his appreciation by turning circles in the dirt. His whole body jigged up and down in merriment, his long arms stretched out and supported on the knuckles of his hands as his white-tufted bottom went round and round.

'Oh, Mum, isn't he adorable?' said Mandy, not taking her eyes off her charge.

Emily Hope smiled. 'I can't argue with you there, love!'

'What plan has Mr Carter made for Jojo?' Mandy asked.

Levina knelt beside Mandy on the grass, hitching up her long, wraparound skirt. 'He's hoping to place him with a surrogate mother,' she replied. 'If we can find a nursing mother out there among the band, we might be able to persuade her to adopt Jojo and care for him as her own.'

'And if you can't?' James ventured.

Mandy suddenly dreaded the answer to James's question.

Levina looked away, her eyes sad. 'Jojo needs other gorillas to learn how to survive. Otherwise, he will never be able to roam the forest in freedom, but will have to fly back to Mr Carter's zoo in England.'

'In that case, we *have* to find him a mum,' Mandy said fiercely. She jumped up. 'Can we introduce him to his nursery now?'

Levina smiled and nodded, so Mandy lifted Jojo gently into her arms. 'Come on, little one. We're going to show you your luxury suite!'

The door to Jojo's hut creaked open and Mandy and James crouched on the floor with him as he crawled about, sniffing with interest, and reached out tiny fingers to touch the branches and leaves. He made noises that sounded like 'hah, hah, hah' and Mandy felt certain he was happy.

'I don't think he'll miss us for a while,' ventured James.

'No, he doesn't even seem aware that we're here,' Mandy replied, smiling. 'That's good. Perhaps he'll curl up and have a sleep.'

They edged slowly out of the hut and closed the door behind them.

That night, Mandy found she was unable to sleep. She kept thinking of Jojo alone in his little room. She got up and slipped out of her hut, closing the woven grass door behind her, then, summoning her courage, began to make her way across the clearing. She could hear the distant howl and hoot of all manner of creatures out there in the forest and it was distinctly creepy – but at least there was a fair amount of light being given off by the full moon.

As she drew near Jojo's hut, Mandy heard him whimpering. She opened the door and moonlight streamed in.

Jojo opened his mouth and screamed, a shrill screech that lasted a full three seconds. He sat in the middle of the floor, looking bewildered.

'Shh! Please, Jojo,' she begged him. 'Come . . . come, Jojo.'

The little gorilla reached up for Mandy's arms, pulled himself up and pushed his soft head up under her chin. He was shaking all over. She soothed him with her hands and he clung to her all the tighter.

'You're coming to sleep with me, Jojo,' Mandy told him. 'You're too little to be out here by yourself. Come on. We'll cuddle up together in my bed.'

# *Three*

Jojo woke Mandy at first light. He had slept with his arms wound round her neck, and his head under her chin. Now he rolled over and lay with his feet in the air, scratching slowly and noisily under each armpit. He plucked at the tapes of his nappy. 'Hah!' he said. 'Hah, hah, oooh.' Then he yawned with a little squeal of satisfaction.

'Had a good night, did you?' Mandy asked him. 'I'm not sure I did, Jojo.' She began to scratch herself and discovered a series of small bites along her collarbone and up under her ear. 'Hmm, fleas. Thanks a lot.'

Jojo lay and watched Mandy pulling on her clothes. When she was dressed, he made a mewling sound and turned down the corners of his mouth. Mandy chuckled. 'Oh, you needn't worry, Jojo. I'm not going to leave you behind!' She gathered him into her arms and stepped out into the harsh morning light.

Mandy found Manou working busily in his kitchen. He was slicing ripe mangoes and papaya into a bowl for breakfast. There was a smell of coffee coming from the gas stove. No one else was up yet. Mandy grinned to herself. A bit different to yesterday morning, she thought.

'*Habari umfaan*,' Manou greeted Mandy, laughingly shaking his head at the sight of Jojo hanging round her neck. He took a small piece of juicy red papaya and offered it to Jojo on the end of his finger. Jojo sniffed, pulled back, sniffed again then gently took Manou's finger into his mouth and sucked.

'Good!' Manou encouraged. '*Mazuri!*'

Mandy planted a kiss on the silky black oval of skin above Jojo's nose. 'I'll make up his bottle, if you like, Manou,' she offered.

She opened the tin of milk powder. Jojo

jigged up and down on her hip, grunting with pleasure, like a small pig.

When the bottle had been prepared, Mandy fed Jojo outside while she waited for the others to wake. The sky to the east was a brilliant gold, streaked with trails of pink and blue, and the sun hadn't yet appeared up above the horizon. The air felt damp and heavy and the ground was dewy underfoot, cool and moist.

'Ready for your forest trek?'

Mandy jumped and looked round. Paul Wilkie, dressed in khaki trousers and heavy boots, stood behind her, admiring the sunrise.

He sat on the grass then began methodically to clean his camera lenses.

'I can't wait,' Mandy told him, then yawned. She was rather sleepy.

But soon afterwards she was revived by another hearty breakfast, during which she told the group about the night she had spent with Jojo.

'I'll give you something to put on those flea bites,' Levina said, smiling.

'You've made a real hit with the young man,' John Carter laughed. Jojo was lying back in Mr Carter's arms, playing with his beard, while

Mandy ate. 'Odd, though,' he mused. 'Jojo didn't complain about sleeping alone when he was in England . . .'

As if to distract his attention from such thoughts, Jojo wrapped his arms round John Carter, said, 'Ooh, ooh,' and buried his face against his neck.

It was time for the visitors' first journey into the forest in search of the gorillas.

Paul Wilkie carried a video camera slung across his back on a broad leather strap, along with an expensive-looking stills camera and an assortment of lenses. Weighted down as he was, Mandy was surprised to see him stride ahead as though he carried nothing at all.

The party followed a single track of flattened grasses that wound its way through the thick undergrowth. There were surface roots to trip them up and thorns to rip at their clothes.

James, walking behind Paul, waved away the platoons of flies that buzzed around him. Mrs Hope had made a little veil of netting and attached it to the brim of her hat to keep the insects off her face.

'You look like you're going to a wedding in

that outfit,' chuckled Mr Hope, slapping at a beetle that had found its way on to his arm.

Jojo sat astride Mandy's hip. He was as light as a doll and held on so tightly that she hardly needed to support him. Hot as she was, she wore a long-sleeved T-shirt and jeans to protect her arms and legs from bites and scratches. Her feet, thrust into boots, felt warm already but she was too excited to mind.

The forest soon thinned and its plant-tangled floor became grassy underfoot. There were groves of palms and huge fig trees that provided welcome shade. A flock of parrots whistled to one another as they flew low over the treetops.

Mandy noticed that Levina and Paul were following markers and direction arrows nailed to the trunks of trees.

'When we reach the river, we'll have a rest,' John Carter called back to the others, wiping his face with a large red handkerchief. There was a screech as a troop of monkeys swung hand to hand through the branches above.

'Colobus!' shouted Paul, training his camera upwards. 'A whole troop of them!'

Jojo jigged fearfully up and down on Mandy's hip, covering his eyes comically with one hand.

Mandy stroked him. 'Don't worry, Jojo. They won't harm you.'

Roused by the sudden activity of the monkeys, a bush-baby screamed, far off, and a wood owl hooted a warning.

'Wow,' said James, craning his neck skywards. 'Wouldn't it be great to have a job like Paul's?' he asked Mandy. He was carrying Paul's binoculars round his neck, along with a hold-all of equipment. 'Earning a living by wandering around the world filming fascinating animals seems a fine way to spend your time.'

'I think you'd have to be very brave to do the job, and strong, too,' Mandy said. 'Just look at all that gear he has to carry!'

Up ahead, Mandy heard the splash of water. They came upon a small, muddy-brown river that snaked its way downhill, tumbling over rocks in its path. The party sank down gratefully on to its grassy banks, ready for a rest.

Emily Hope took off her hat and retied her hair, which was damp with the effort of her walking.

James sank down beside Mandy and untied his bootlaces. 'Phew, it's hot.' He tickled Jojo under the chin.

But Jojo was concentrating on the large, shiny, metal button he'd discovered on Mandy's jeans. He sat on Mandy's lap, tugging at the button.

'Do you think he would let me hold him?' James asked, wistfully. 'He's become very attached to you, hasn't he?'

'Yes,' Mandy agreed. 'But you take a turn when we set off again, OK?' She smiled at James. His freckles were turning darker in the sun.

Levina distributed iced water from a flask to everyone in tiny plastic cups, then handed Jojo a bottle.

Jojo crawled off Mandy's lap and lay on his back on the grass and took hold of his bottle with his agile feet, sucking at it noisily.

Paul took out a penknife and sliced up several apples, on to which he sprinkled a little salt from a tiny packet in his pocket.

'Salt?' Mandy said, puzzled. 'On apples?'

'Very good for you in this heat,' Paul replied. 'The body loses salt when you perspire, you see.'

The apples were sharp-tasting, but good – though Jojo didn't like his one bit, and spat it out rather rudely.

Levina said it was time to go on and

everybody put their boots back on and struggled to their feet.

In order to entice Jojo away from Mandy, James tapped on the row of small metal buttons at the opening of his shirt. Jojo was entranced, first by the sound they made, then by the fact that they were sparkling silver in the sunlight. He inclined his head and reached out a finger, curiously. James lifted him into his arms and the little ape settled happily against his chest, one long arm looped round James's neck, his fingers playing and pulling at the buttons.

The party moved on. After a while, a sudden sound tore through the trees above their heads. Mandy thought at first that it was a mighty clap of thunder, but as everyone looked up at the sky, they were surprised to see a vast flock of large birds rise as one from their perches and take off, squawking. The combined flapping of hundreds of pairs of wings was ear-splitting.

For a second, Jojo froze in terror in James's arms. Then, in sudden panic, he wrenched himself free and leaped up and on to an overhanging branch of a huge umbrella-shaped tree.

'Jojo!' James yelled.

Mandy, who was still staring at the amazing sight of the birds in the sky, spun round. She followed James's dismayed gaze and saw the little gorilla up in the tree. He had clambered well out of their reach and lay clutching weakly at a thin branch.

'Oh, Jojo!' Mandy repeated, more softly. She looked at John Carter. 'What do we do now?'

'Sorry,' mumbled James. He took off his glasses and wiped them on his shirt. Jojo had used his nose as a springboard when he had jumped into the tree and the glasses had dropped to James's chin.

'Not your fault, lad,' said Mr Carter, putting his hand on James's shoulder. 'Now, how to get the little devil down, that's the question . . .'

'Paul,' said Adam suddenly, 'can I stand on your shoulders? I could reach him then.'

'Sure. It's worth a try,' Paul replied.

It took several tries before Adam found his balance. Paul staggered around under Adam Hope's weight and tipped him off twice, but eventually, with John Carter holding on to him, they managed.

Mandy saw that Jojo was trembling all over. He clung tightly on to the branch, looking down at the ground so very far away, and his round brown eyes seemed to bore into Mandy's. 'Help me, please,' he seemed to be saying.

Mr Hope, his arms outspread for balance like an acrobat, lunged up at Jojo's feet. The little gorilla let out a shriek of alarm and edged higher up the branch.

'Um, I don't expect you're up to shinning up a tree, are you, John?' Emily Hope asked Mr Carter.

'I confess I am not, nowadays,' Mr Carter replied, grinning a little sheepishly.

'In that case, if anyone is going to be able to get Jojo down,' Mrs Hope concluded, 'it will have to be you, Mandy. Jojo seems to have bonded with you since the night you took him into your hut!'

Mandy nodded.

'I suppose *you* want to stand on me now?' Paul joked, pretending to be hard-done-by.

Mandy grinned as she stepped up on to Paul's braced thigh then stepped up on to his shoulders, her fingers gripping his hair.

'Ouch, ooch . . .' he complained.

'Sorry!' Mandy slowly gained balance and stood upright. Jojo was well out of her reach.

She held up her arms to him and he looked at her soulfully with fearful eyes and made a chittering noise. 'Come, Jojo . . . come along to me . . .' Mandy pleaded.

Jojo was far too frightened to jump into Mandy's arms. 'Can you get me near there?' she asked Paul, pointing to the fork of two branches. 'Then I'll climb up and get him.'

Mandy was shaking as she heaved herself up into the big branches of the leafy tree. She gripped the bark with her knees and edged along and upwards, talking softly to Jojo all the time, until she could reach out and touch his fur.

Jojo twisted round to make certain it really was Mandy, then flung out one little arm and took hold of her hand. She pulled him gently off the branch and against her chest. Jojo jigged frantically and screamed loudly in relief. 'Shhh!' she begged him. 'It's OK now. You're safe!'

Mandy edged her way back the way she had come, with Jojo clinging on to her back, his arms tight round her throat. When she reached the fork in the tree Mandy slithered down on her tummy until she felt the tips of her toes touch Paul's solid shoulders.

'I've got you,' Emily Hope said, reaching up

for Mandy's hands. 'Well done. And here's one young gorilla who won't be interested in climbing trees for quite a while!'

With Jojo firmly astride Mandy's hip, they set off once more.

The grass soon became waist high and waved in the breeze like a show of hands at a football match. Elephant grass, Mandy had heard it called.

Levina signalled to everyone to stop. She paused, then looked questioningly at John Carter. He nodded, and Levina gave a 'thumbs-up' sign to Paul, who then hauled the video camera on to his shoulder and began to film her.

Levina spoke softly into the tiny microphone clipped on to her shirtfront. 'We have made our way to the area where the group – or band – of gorillas we are watching have most likely spent the night,' she began.

'There's a powerful smell in the vicinity and we should come across their night nests any moment . . .' Levina had begun to record her video documentary.

They continued slowly for a few metres,

before coming upon several large, neat circles worn into the floor of a flattened area of grass, each of them showing clearly the outline of a huge and heavy body. Above the circles, flies cruised lazily.

'We've found them,' Levina breathed into her microphone. 'This is their night nesting area. The band will be nearby.'

Mandy's excitement mounted. She was hot and tired, and her feet hurt, but she wouldn't have traded places with anyone in the world at that moment.

'We're going to move on now to see if we can spot the band resting or feeding,' Levina said into the camera. She signalled to the group to move on.

They continued slowly, for another twenty minutes or so, until the floor of the forest became dim and cool once again. The musty smell of rotting leaves and mud was almost overpowering now, but the shade of the forest was so welcome it didn't seem to matter.

Suddenly, Levina stopped again. The rest of the party followed suit. Mandy looked, but all she could see was the dense vegetation surrounding them.

John Carter touched Mandy's shoulder and silently pointed over to their left. Mandy turned and, through the undergrowth, caught a glimpse of a black, domed head. She willed her loudly hammering heart to be still and took a deep breath to calm herself, the way she'd seen her mother do during tense moments in the surgery at home.

The party edged slowly closer, until a young gorilla came clearly into view. He was sitting at the base of a fig tree, sorting methodically through the seeds of ripe, red fruit. Then Mandy realised that he was not alone. Other gorillas were sitting and resting against the spread-out, lower branches of the tree. They looked over, blinking with interest, but showed no inclination to move or investigate the party of visitors.

'They are quite used to people now,' Levina whispered. 'They won't bother with us.' She signalled to Paul to begin filming again, then began reporting their find into her microphone, her eyes never leaving the gorillas . . .

'This is the little band we've been following. They've become quite used to our presence. The leader, or alpha male, we call Domino.

He's getting on in years now and is just about ready, we think, to give up his position of dominance . . .'

Mandy studied the elderly gorilla that Levina must be talking about. His hair had become stringy and grey in colour, and the top of his head was now bald. But he was still powerful looking.

Mr Hope put his hands on Mandy's shoulders. 'Pretty big!' he whispered.

Levina turned off her microphone and pointed to the huge old gorilla. 'Domino would weigh in at around 200 kilos!' she informed them.

Mandy nodded, her heart thudding inside her chest with a mixture of fear and delight. What would they do if Domino suddenly decided to object to their presence after all, and charged at them?

She counted seven other gorillas of varying sizes. The band made a peaceful picture as they sat there, calmly ripping and tearing at fruit and bark with their hands and teeth.

Mandy's eye was caught by a young gorilla clambering in the lower branches of the fig tree. She could see that he was interested in something on the trunk – probably an insect of some kind. He bent to sniff at it, and traced its path along the bark with an outstretched finger. But suddenly the gorilla seemed to tumble out of the tree.

Mandy gasped as she watched him somersault to the ground – then gasped again as he rushed over, flung himself at one of the bigger gorillas, then ran away, shrieking with delight at his prank.

The adult gorilla, annoyed at the interruption, swatted at the young gorilla's head, missed, and toppled comically over on to his side.

Mandy shoulders shook with silent laughter. 'They're so human!' she whispered.

'Aren't they?' John Carter agreed, smiling.

There was a soft whirring sound coming from Paul's camera, but the noise didn't seem to bother the gorillas. The big lens moved back and forth across the group, zooming in close one moment and pulling back for a wider shot the next.

Levina pointed to the other gorillas in turn. 'That's an older female, Theresa . . . with her young daughter Cha Cha . . . and the smaller one there is a male, Bruno, the son of the female with the brownish fur, up against the trunk.'

'But none of the band looks a likely surrogate mother for our little friend here,' John Carter whispered. He was clearly disappointed.

Jojo continued to sleep, unaware, in Mandy's arms.

'Hang on, though – look!' Mrs Hope said. 'Up there, in the lower branches . . .'

Everyone craned their necks to see what she had spotted.

Only just visible through the shadowy screen of leaves, a large gorilla sat hunched against the trunk, knees drawn up, head lolling wearily.

Levina put her binoculars to her eyes and trained them on the gorilla. Then, after a few seconds, and without saying a word, she passed them on to Mandy, who was right beside her.

Much of the gorilla's large body was obscured, but, as Mandy watched, the gorilla yawned, then scratched what had to be the most enormous belly Mandy had ever seen. 'Oh!' she said, still peering. 'This one in the tree . . . I think it . . . I mean she . . . must be . . . She's going to have a baby!'

# *Four*

Levina strained forward, a look of excitement on her face. 'I've never seen her before!' she breathed. 'She must have arrived recently, wanting to attach herself to this band. How wonderful!' She looked at John Carter. 'What do you think?' she asked.

He nodded, thoughtfully. 'She could be just what Jojo needs,' he replied slowly. He looked at the tiny gorilla, and then at Mandy. 'Let's hope so,' he smiled.

'We must name her,' Paul said, from behind his lens. 'Anyone got any ideas?'

'Grace,' suggested Adam Hope immediately.

'She's hardly graceful in that advanced state of pregnancy, I know, but she may just turn out to be Jojo's saving grace.'

'I like that,' smiled Emily Hope. Everyone else nodded enthusiastically.

'So do I,' said Levina. 'Then Grace it is.' She took out her notebook and began scribbling in tiny, rapid handwriting, documenting details about the gorilla's size, shape and colouring.

Grace looked around her through lazy, half-closed eyelids. She let her head fall back against the trunk, and rolled it slowly from side to side. Then she began carefully to manoeuvre herself down from her perch on the branch.

She waited beside the massive tree trunk, partially hidden from view, patiently watching Domino and the others.

Domino eyed Grace a little fiercely, then slowly ambled over to her.

Mandy caught her breath. He appeared so threatening that Mandy was afraid he might try to hurt Grace.

The huge old gorilla squatted beside Grace, who turned her head away, adopting a non-threatening posture, and looked down at her belly.

For what seemed a long time, Domino stood over the newcomer, as though making up his mind what to do with her. Then, as though finally satisfied, Domino turned away and slowly made his way back to the band.

'That's a relief,' said James softly. 'I thought he might thump her!'

Levina turned to John Carter. 'I can't get a clear enough view of that belly now, but from my first impression when she was in the tree, I would say she is almost ready to give birth.'

John Carter nodded his agreement.

Mandy realised that her arms were aching from having held on to Jojo for such a long time. She could hardly feel her fingers; they were numb from being still. But she dared not lay him down – and she didn't want to miss watching this fantastic scene being played out before them.

'Isn't it amazing to think that we're watching for real what's going to be a television film?' she whispered to James.

James nodded without moving his eyes from Domino and Grace.

Suddenly, there was an explosion of loud

hooting and barking. It came from a little way off, to the left.

Domino immediately turned towards the noise. He clenched his fists and drummed long and loudly on his barrel chest, making a hollow booming sound that could surely be heard the length and breadth of the forest.

The noise woke Jojo. He blinked, then fearfully scrabbled up Mandy until his head was pressed right under her chin. He squeezed his eyes tightly shut. Mandy was terrified herself, but, holding Jojo closely to her, she looked to Levina for direction.

Levina held up a hand to warn the party to keep very still.

Two young gorillas burst into the clearing, hunched over in full gallop, leaping and shrieking at each other, and baring their fearsome teeth. They tore about in a frenzy of fury, hammering on trees with their fists and ripping up the foliage that they grabbed as they ran.

Mandy covered Jojo's eyes with her hand, just in case he decided to open them, and panicked at what was happening in front of them.

Paul's camera had hummed into action again.

Over the noise of the gorilla display, Levina talked as loudly as she dared into her microphone. 'These two males are Bruno and Kima – Kima is the heavier one,' she explained to her invisible audience. 'There have been rumblings between them for some time. It's likely that they are fighting for dominance; to see who will take over leadership of the group when Domino is no longer up to the job, or dies.'

While the screaming and whooping of the display continued, Mandy noticed Grace shuffle awkwardly behind the tree, out of sight.

Domino presided over the fight like a referee in a boxing ring. He paced this way and that, tense and alert, watching every move of the young males.

But finally, Bruno, the shorter and less powerfully-built gorilla, was forced to concede defeat. He backed off, shaking his head as if dizzy, using a big fist to wipe one of his eyes. The lid had been torn and was bleeding. The injured gorilla retreated away from the clearing until he was gone from view.

Domino went over and sniffed the victorious Kima. Then he sat down and looked long and hard after Bruno.

'Poor Bruno,' Mandy said. 'He was hurt.' She looked at Levina. 'What will happen to him now?' she asked.

Levina smiled at Mandy's sad expression. 'I expect Domino will allow him to come back, once he's had a little time to lick his wounds and nurse his injured pride,' she said. 'But now Bruno has lost the fight for leadership here, he needs to be looking elsewhere . . .'

'Well, I'm rather glad the fighting's over, fascinating though it was!' exclaimed Mrs Hope, standing from her cramped posture with difficulty.

'Me too,' said James, wiping his face with his sleeve. 'Where did Paul go?'

Just then, Paul's voice came floating down from a tree behind them, making James jump. 'What about that!' Paul said. 'I got it all on film. Fantastic stuff.'

'It certainly was,' agreed John Carter. 'I haven't been so close to a display like that for years!' he added.

'Are you all right, love?' Emily Hope said to Mandy, who hadn't said anything. 'You've been such a dedicated mother to that little gorilla, you must be tired.'

'I'm fine,' Mandy reassured her mother, though she had probably never been so excited and scared in her life! And she was sure she'd never been as hot. 'But I could do with a drink,' she added.

'I think everyone could,' Levina agreed.' And then we'll head back into camp. We've had an excellent day. And coming across Grace was a real bonus!'

'She's treat, isn't she?' Paul said. 'Let's just hope she ends up staying with this band, and that we can interest her in Jojo. If not, Mandy will be stuck with him for life!'

As the party made its way back to Camp Kahuzi, Mandy asked John Carter what would happen now.

'Well, there's no guarantee that Grace will stay with our band of gorillas, of course,' Mr Carter said cautiously. 'We must remember that. But as she is about to give birth, and Domino seems to have accepted her, it seems quite likely that she will stay around.' He smiled. 'So now we must wait for Grace to have her infant. Then she will start producing milk – hopefully, enough for two!'

Mr Carter dabbed at his flushed face with his handkerchief, then continued: 'I expect Grace will have found herself a comfortable and safe place nearby for the coming birth. That's where she'll have gone now. If we are lucky enough to locate her haven, then this will be the best place to take Jojo, when the time is right.'

'I think I'll have a scout round for Grace, now,' Paul Wilkie said. He still looked as fresh as when they'd started out that morning. Mandy marvelled at his stamina. 'It would save us a lot of time if we know exactly where to go with Jojo later,' Paul continued.

'Sure, if you're up to it,' John Carter replied.

'Right, I'll catch up with you later,' Paul said, already forging a path through the dense green bush.

Back at Camp Kahuzi, Manou produced a pile of sandwiches and cold lemonade. After they had eaten, John Carter took Jojo off to play in the 'nursery' for a while.

'Why don't you two go off and have a swim?' Levina suggested to Mandy and James. 'There's a water hole just to the west of the camp that is quite safe.'

'Sounds brilliant,' said James enthusiastically. 'I'll just go to the tent and get my . . . oh! here's Paul.'

Paul Wilkie was grinning, dabbing at the perspiration streaming from his temples and upper lip. His forearms were covered in bleeding scratches, which he appeared not to notice.

'You look like you've got good news,' guessed Levina.

Paul nodded, then sat down and helped himself to a drink. 'Grace has set up in a small glade just north of the rest of the band. She's built her night nest there. Very cosy.' He swigged deeply from his glass.

'Could you take us to it . . . find it again, I mean?' Mandy said.

'With my eyes closed,' smiled Paul, eyeing the now-empty plate. 'Got any more of those sandwiches, Manou?'

'Wow, well done,' James said admiringly. 'Come on, Mandy, let's go and have that swim now, before it gets too late.'

Kadebe acted as guide and led Mandy and James along an overgrown path to where a

circle of inviting-looking water sparkled in the
sun. It was all that remained of a once fast-
flowing river that had long since dried up.

They ducked under drooping palm-fronds,
and gazed in wonder at the towering glossy-
green plant life they had to skirt around to reach
the pool. Mud as dark as chocolate lay thick
along its edges. Branches, torn from trees by
storms, had been stripped of leaves and bark
and tossed on to the shore, where they lay
partially embedded, bleached a scary white by
the vicious sun.

'Ugh, they look like skeletons,' said James.

Kadebe led them to where a section of
the water lay protected by a semi-circle of
large, smooth rocks. Using the long stick he
carried for support, Kadebe stepped up and
then squatted on the biggest of the bulging
rocks, watching over the pool for signs of
danger.

After a minute or so, he said, 'Swim
now,' and grinned. 'Safe for swim. Kadebe say
so.'

Mandy and James needed no further
encouragement. They took off their boots and
hats and plunged in, squealing loudly at the

shock of the cold water, which they hadn't, somehow, expected.

'Much rain last week,' Kadebe advised them. 'Make water fresh; make water cold.'

They enjoyed the pool for the best part of an hour. Kadebe puffed at a long pipe of tobacco, gazing from his rock perch across the canopy of the forest, before he gave in to the intense afternoon heat, and dozed off to the peaceful sound of birdcall and splashing.

None of them noticed the sky darkening, changing dramatically and quickly from a cheerful bright blue to shades of charcoal and plum. The shadow of the stormy sky fell over the pool, blotting out the light from the sun in seconds.

Kadebe woke and motioned with an urgent hand for James and Mandy to get out. They clambered up the rocks as the first giant spots of rain began to fall. It was like being pelted with small stones.

'Ouch,' said James, scrambling into his boots. 'Let's get out of here. Quick, Mandy.' He bent to tie up the lace of her left boot, while Mandy fumbled with the right.

Kadebe shuffled from foot to foot impatiently, fearful of the lightning that was certain to follow, and anxious to get them to safety.

The heavens opened. The sky seemed to blacken, then crack open and empty itself on their heads. Small hailstones stung their cheeks as they ran, clumsily, tripping over roots on the forest floor.

Kadebe smacked at the trees with his stick, wielding a path that sent the raindrops flying and intensified the soaking they were getting. Then, just as they were clear of the trees, a shattering bolt of lightning tore through the sky, like a hundred flashbulbs going off in their faces. It lit up the camp like a beam from a powerful torch, and Mandy could see her father standing in the door of his hut, scanning the gloom, anxiety etched on his face.

'We're here,' she shouted. 'Here, Dad, don't worry . . .'

They dashed over to the hut, shouting their thanks to Kadebe as he rushed off to his own shelter. Emily Hope stood there with towels for them.

James crashed through the door after Mandy. 'Wow,' he said. 'Who needed a swim . . .?'

Later, as they sat round the kitchen with a pot of strong, hot tea, John Carter announced, 'I'm a little worried about Jojo; he just doesn't seem himself. He wouldn't drink his milk this afternoon, doesn't seem interested in fruit, either – and he's running a slight temperature too, I think.'

Mandy sat bolt upright in her chair. 'Can I go and see him?'

'Too much lightning, still,' Manou warned. 'You wait,' he said, topping up the teapot with boiling water.

'Manou is right,' agreed Levina. 'That lightning can be dangerous – even between here and Jojo's hut.'

Mandy sipped her tea. Her hair was still plastered wetly to her cheeks. Out of the window she could see steam rise like smoke from a bonfire as the heat from the late afternoon sun strained through the purple-streaked sky and beamed down its warmth on the soggy earth. She longed to see Jojo. But she would have to wait.

# Five

When, at last, the sky began to lighten, Mandy and James dashed across the waterlogged clearing to Jojo's hut. Pushing open the door, Mandy saw several large lizards and geckos scramble up the whitewashed walls for cover and vanish like magic into the thatch of the roof.

Jojo was lying on the little pile of sacks and straw that made up his bed. He lay on his back, idly fingering Levina's bead necklace, and didn't move or make a noise when Mandy called to him. He simply turned his head and gazed at her with such an expression of sadness in his chocolate-coloured eyes that Mandy's heart turned right over.

James crouched down and stroked the baby gorilla's hairy tummy. 'How are you feeling, Jojo?' he asked.

The baby gorilla belched delicately and, with a flicker of interest, took off James's glasses. He examined them, then sighed and tossed them backwards over his shoulder.

'Hey!' exclaimed James, groping for them in the straw.

'Nothing seems to interest him,' said Mandy, concerned.

'How does he look?' John Carter's voice came from the doorway.

Mandy and James glanced up. Mandy shook her head. 'He seems . . . sort of . . . sad,' she said.

Emily Hope followed Mr Carter into the room. 'Move over a bit, love,' she said. 'Let me have a look at him.' She eased down into the straw beside Jojo.

John Carter took up position on the other side of the low sack bed.

Jojo allowed Mrs Hope to look at his gums and the whites of his eyes and, while being distracted by Mr Carter's shiny gold wristwatch, had his temperature taken. Bored with the watch, he reached up and seized Emily Hope's ponytail, which he tugged on rather listlessly, then did the same to Mr Carter's beard.

Mr Carter put his face to Jojo's and rubbed his heart-shaped black nose with his own. But Jojo showed no inclination to rise from the bed and crawl into the arms of the only real security he had known since his birth.

'Hmm,' said Emily Hope, frowning. 'There's a bit of conjunctivitis in his eyes – just a mild infection – but I'm certain that Jojo isn't seriously sick . . . no parasites in his coat . . . a bit dehydrated, maybe.'

It saddened Mandy to think that Jojo could be unhappy in the little haven they had created for him.

John Carter saw her expression and seemed to guess her thoughts. 'It's nothing that we – or you – haven't done, Mandy, my dear,' he said kindly. 'No baby gorilla could have had better care than Jojo has had. But gorillas are highly intelligent animals and family life is very important to them. My guess is that he's pining for a life that he senses is out there in the forest somewhere; for a sense of belonging, of family . . . Jojo wants to be a gorilla. He wants to be with his own species.'

'Especially after he smelled the family of gorillas out there in the forest earlier . . . maybe that's what started him pining,' James suggested.

'So what can we do?' Mandy asked anxiously.

'Well . . .' With difficulty, John Carter got to his feet and rearranged his tangled beard with his fingertips, 'First of all, we have to get some liquid into the little fellow, or he will start to weaken pretty quickly, isn't that so, Emily?'

Emily Hope nodded. She was stroking Jojo's forehead.

'Then,' Mr Carter went on determinedly, 'we've got to do our utmost to find Jojo a gorilla mother as soon as possible. The last thing I want is to have to take Jojo back to England. There's no suitable surrogate mother for him in the zoo right now, and I'm quite certain his mother isn't going to have a change of heart.'

'Grace,' said Mandy softly. 'She's our only hope.'

Mr Carter nodded. 'It looks that way,' he replied. 'But, Mandy,' he warned, gently, 'we still have a long way to go. There are all sorts of things that might go wrong. Grace might decide she doesn't want Jojo, just as his natural mother did.'

Mandy's face fell. She couldn't bear the thought of that. *Oh, Grace*, she pleaded silently, *please don't let us down. Jojo needs you!*

Mandy could hardly sleep that night, and Jojo didn't even seem to want to leave his den to sleep in her bed.

The following morning Mandy rushed over to see how he had fared during the night.

John Carter and Levina were already there with him. The tiny gorilla looked listless and miserable.

'We really need to tempt this little chap into eating something,' Mr Carter said. 'However it turns out, he'll need all of his strength.'

Levina went over to Manou in the kitchen and returned with Jojo's bottle and some crushed banana leaves on a plate. 'Do you want to try, Mandy?' she asked.

Mandy put her hands into the juicy mess on the plate and tried to get Jojo to suck her fingers, but he turned his head. He showed the same indifference to the bottle of milk.

'He really doesn't seem interested at all, does

he?' Adam Hope observed. He and Mrs Hope
had come in to check on Jojo. 'He seems to be
losing strength rather quickly, too.'

'And that eye looks as if it will need an
antibiotic ointment,' added Emily Hope.

'The problem is,' Levina said frustratedly,
'we've got antibiotic in injection and powder
form here at the camp, but not as an ointment.
I wouldn't expect to get close enough to use an
ointment on a gorilla out here, so didn't stock
up on the ointment Jojo needs!'

'Can't we use the powder – put some in his
milk, or something?' James asked.

'Not really, no,' Emily Hope told him. 'We
need to treat the eye directly.'

'I have an idea,' John Carter said, slowly. 'I
need to go into Ebola to make a few telephone
calls today. I could pick up some antibiotic
ointment for Jojo's eye from the pharmacy . . .
But I could also take Jojo to Makezi Umpondo.

'Dr Umpondo is an African zoologist,' Mr
Carter explained. 'He has studied the local
lowland gorillas for years, and knows as much
about them as anyone. But he has also gained
an equally impressive knowledge of local
herbal medicine. I've known him to produce

astounding remedies over the years. His potions seem to go beyond the bounds of science! He might know a way to keep Jojo going, until Grace is ready for him.'

Levina nodded enthusiastically. 'Dr Umpondo has been out here a couple of times since I arrived. A great man! Let's give it a try.' She thought for a second. 'I need to stock up on some supplies, too. Why don't we all go into town after breakfast?'

'Suits me,' said Adam Hope. 'I'd like to put a call through to Animal Ark and see how Simon's coping in the surgery without us.'

It was decided that they'd all pile into the camp truck and Kadebe would drive them the twenty kilometres or so to the town of Ebola.

After breakfast, Mandy collected Jojo and sat up with him in the cab of the truck, sandwiched between John Carter and James. Paul Wilkie had come for the ride and shared the back seats with Mr and Mrs Hope and Levina.

The truck lurched along the potholed roads, churning up great clouds of red dust as it went, eventually arriving in the outskirts of Ebola. In wide dirt streets with muddy gutters, brown-skinned children played football with tin cans and swung on car tyres hanging from ropes.

The truck passed a shaded open market. Vendors squatted comfortably next to their wares: pineapples and oranges stacked in towering triangles; maize cobs piled in their green sheaths; huge bunches of bananas; smoked fish, nuts and grass matting; stumpy white candles and cooking oils.

Kadebe parked the truck in the middle of town and, while the others went off to sort out their various bits of business, Mandy and James stayed in the truck with Kadebe and the weak and dozing Jojo.

It was boiling hot in the cab and they were relieved when the others returned.

'Right,' said Adam Hope. 'First things first: let's get some of this antibiotic cream on to Jojo's eye.' He took out a small tube from a bag of shopping. 'Now, hold him firmly, Mandy, so that he doesn't wriggle, and tip him backwards a little – that's right . . .' As Mandy did as she was asked, Mr Hope smoothed some ointment on to the sore eye.

Jojo flinched and blinked up at the big man above him. 'Hah, eeh,' he said, softly.

Mr Hope smiled. 'OK, little one. That's

enough for the time being. Now let's try and get your other problem sorted out.' He looked at John Carter.

The older man nodded. 'Dr Umpondo's house, then.'

Leaving Kadebe with the truck, the party followed John Carter through the crowded streets, attracting curious stares from the local people.

The bungalow he led them to was painted a cheerful buttercup yellow. Resting on the veranda, a large man in snow-white trousers and shirt was reading a journal, a big glass jug of lemonade and ice on a table beside him. Seeing it, Mandy's mouth watered.

'Hello there,' Mr Carter called.

Makezi Umpondo put down his journal and stood up, a look of surprised pleasure on his face. 'My friend! You are back with us in Africa once again. It is good to see you!' Putting his hands on John Carter's shoulders, he gave them an affectionate squeeze, then did the same with Levina.

After everyone had been introduced, more glasses and further supplies of ice-cold lemonade were fetched.

'And now, tell me, who is this little fellow?' Dr Umpondo asked, peering at Jojo. 'He looks a little sorry for himself.'

Jojo hid his face in Mandy's neck, while John Carter explained Jojo's situation.

Dr Umpondo let out a long, slow sigh. 'Gorillas are emotional animals – very sensitive. They don't thrive well when separated from their own kind. I have known infant gorillas that have become separated from their mothers to die of grief. They lost the will to live and refused to eat.'

Mandy's heart grew heavy as she listened. She wouldn't be able to bear it if that happened to Jojo. She looked at James. He had turned pale at what Dr Umpondo had just said.

'We have identified a pregnant female on the reserve,' John Carter continued. 'She is due to give birth any time now and we're hoping she'll then be prepared to take Jojo on, too.'

'She will certainly be more receptive to Jojo when she is in milk, with an infant of her own to care for,' agreed Dr Umpondo.

'But if we can't get Jojo to eat and drink, we might lose him before we have the chance to offer him to Grace,' John Carter concluded gravely.

Dr Umpondo looked at Jojo long and hard. 'Almost five months old, right?' John Carter nodded and coaxed Jojo into turning around.

'So, young man, you need a little help, eh?' Dr Umpondo crooned.

Jojo looked back at him, solemnly.

Dr Umpondo stood up. 'Come this way,' he said. 'Let's see what we can find.'

They followed Dr Umpondo through the house, into a small, gloomy study, lined with large volumes of books. He went about opening the blinds and sunlight flooded into the room and illuminated several strangely shaped glass bottles and jars, crowded into cabinets.

Dr Umpondo put on a pair of spectacles and peered closely at the tiny handwriting on each of the labels, selecting some and rejecting others, saying to himself, 'Aha, this will do . . . and this . . . and a drop or two of that . . .'

James looked at Mandy and wrinkled his nose. 'Do you think it's safe? That stuff he's mixing, I mean?' he whispered. He nodded in the direction of the sludge-coloured liquids in the bottles.

'I'm sure he must know what he's doing,' Mandy whispered back.

'Bring the young man over to me, Mandy,' the big man boomed, removing his glasses. 'I have made up a tonic that might make him feel a little better in himself.'

Mandy took Jojo over and, holding him in the crook of her arm, tipped him backwards. One little fist clutched at her shirt.

Dr Umpondo hovered over Jojo, holding a syringe without a needle, into which he'd put the herbal tonic mixture. Mandy's nose began to twitch. The mixture smelled foul! Her heart sank again. Jojo had turned up his nose at milk and fresh fruit, so how was Dr Umpondo going to get him to swallow something much less appetising?

Jojo's nose began to twitch, too. Dr Umpondo grinned. 'I can see the doubt in your face, Mandy,' he said. 'But trust me, the little one will love it.'

He quickly opened Jojo's mouth and shot the thick, dark liquid in the syringe to the side of the gorilla's cheek.

Jojo's eyes widened in surprise, and he swallowed. Then, with his free arm – the one that wasn't pinned against Mandy – he reached up, seized the empty syringe and popped it back into his mouth.

Mandy laughed in delight. 'There's no more,' she told him. 'It's all gone.'

Jojo sucked furiously on the end of the empty syringe, then held it to his eye. Disappointed, he flung it to the floor, turned his face to Mandy and gave a big sigh.

'Well, that wasn't too hard!' said Emily Hope, smiling. 'I wish all my patients were so keen on taking their medicine!'

Dr Umpondo picked up the discarded

syringe. 'Now, you're going to need this, little man,' he said. 'Otherwise you won't be able to have more of your medicine later on.'

Jojo lifted his lips at Dr Umpondo. 'Ooh,' he said, and put one small finger into Mandy's right nostril, seeming a little brighter already.

Dr Umpondo smiled at Mandy. 'You can take your charge home now – and teach him some manners!'

Mandy nodded her thanks, then forced herself to ask: 'Dr Umpondo, do you think Grace – the female gorilla we found in the forest – will look after Jojo?'

The big man leaned back against his worktable and folded his arms across his chest. 'It would be a wonderful thing, if this were to happen. But, as I am sure John and Levina have already said, it is by no means definite that she will. It is always a gamble . . . and if she doesn't . . .'

'Yes, what if Grace decides she doesn't want him?' James asked, in a hollow voice. 'Might she . . . harm him?'

'That is unlikely,' Dr Umpondo replied. 'Jojo is not a threat to her, you see. No, my guess is that she will either take him on, or take her own infant and simply walk away.'

The thought of Jojo being rejected again brought tears to Mandy's eyes. It would break his heart – and hers, she thought. She put her cheek against Jojo's soft fur and he disentangled one long arm from round her neck and stuck the tip of his finger into her mouth.

'I'm sorry to shock you with the facts, 'Dr Umpondo said kindly, as he showed them out. 'I see I have made you sad. But we have done what we can for the little fellow. Let us hope that he will be one of our success stories – that one day, he might walk free through the forest, with offspring of his own.'

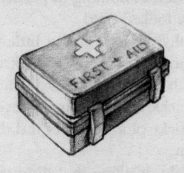

## Six

The cab of the truck was like an oven when they got back to it. John Carter had gone back to the post office to make a second telephone call to England, and Levina advised them to wait for him under the shade of a nearby tree.

Mandy passed the time watching a group of children who were sitting and plaiting palm-fronds into necklaces and decorative headgear.

'I'm back!' boomed John Carter, striding towards them. 'Sorry to have kept you hanging about in this heat.' Mr Carter looked grim as he heaved himself into the cab. He said very little during the journey, preferring to gaze out of the window at nothing in particular. Mandy thought he looked tired.

Thankfully, Jojo seemed a little livelier. He sat on Mandy's lap in the truck and busied himself with things on the dashboard, then the seat-belt buckle and its strap. His eye was gooey with the sticky ointment, but it didn't seem to bother him.

'Fancy Jojo drinking that disgusting-looking stuff Dr Umpondo made for him,' said James, wrinkling his nose.

'It didn't smell much better, either,' Mandy laughed. 'But it obviously tastes great to Jojo – and it seems like it's done him good.'

To James's delight, Jojo crawled across the passenger seat to his lap, reached up one long arm and tousled his hair affectionately, saying, 'Hah, eee, eee, hah.' He then covered his eyes with his hands, as though he were having a great laugh at James's expense.

Mandy reached over and kissed Jojo's nose. More than anything she wanted Jojo to get well, and stay well, until he had found another mother.

To everyone's delight, Jojo had eagerly taken a

bottle and a few slivers of fruit when they had arrived back at camp. It seemed that, at least for the time being, he was safe again.

But, during supper that evening, John Carter announced that he would have to leave Camp Kahuzi the following afternoon.

'So soon?' asked Levina, surprised. 'Why? Has there been bad news?'

Mr Carter shook his head, then began to explain. 'For a long time, I have been negotiating with a zoo in the United States to let me have a young male gorilla called Targa, on loan, as a mate for one of my female gorillas. When I called England from Ebola this morning, I found out that they have finally organised for him to come. It's a very exciting prospect indeed – but he is due to arrive in only two days' time!'

Mr Carter looked around at everyone listening. 'I must be there to settle him in, of course.'

Mandy was dismayed. 'But . . . Jojo . . . You won't . . . will you be taking him back with you?' she asked, dreading his answer.

Mr Carter smiled. 'Had it not been for the timely visit of you good people here in Camp

Kahuzi, I most certainly would have had to take Jojo back to England tomorrow.' He looked at Levina and Paul, then continued: 'I know how busy Levina and Paul are, making their television documentary, so I could not have left Jojo in their care until Grace was ready. However,' Mr Carter went on, 'as Jojo seems to have found splendid carers in Mandy and James, I feel able to entrust him to them, until the time is right. That is, if everyone agrees,' he finished, looking at the faces around the table.

Everyone nodded in approval.

'We'll do our absolute best for him, Mr Carter,' Mandy said, looking at James.

'Of course we will,' James agreed. 'But . . . what will happen if Grace does reject Jojo?' he asked, worriedly.

'Then I will arrange for Jojo to come back to England,' Mr Carter replied. 'In the meantime, as a last resort, I will start looking around for a suitable long-term foster mother for him – a human one.'

Straight away, Mandy wanted to volunteer, to tell Mr Carter that she would keep Jojo at home in Welford after their return, but she knew this to be an impossible suggestion. Welford was too far from Mr Carter's zoo, and anyway, she and James would be back in school.

Besides, Mandy knew in her heart that, although Jojo had taken to her, if he were able to choose between having a human or a gorilla mother, he would choose his own species every time. No, she would just have to hope that Jojo would be able to stay with Grace.

After supper, Mandy changed Jojo's nappy. Then, using the syringe tube that Dr Umpondo had given them, she sucked up the dark liquid mixture from the bottle.

Jojo's intelligent eyes watched her every move. 'Hah! Oooh!' he said, and jigged a little to show his approval.

'He's certainly a good patient,' said James as he watched.

Mandy laughed as Jojo lay back in her arms, making small slurping sounds and smacking his eager lips together. 'He loves this icky stuff! Now, open wide!' she told him. Holding the syringe between her forefinger and middle finger, she inserted the plastic tip into Jojo's mouth.

He began to suck noisily as Mandy squeezed down gently and the syrupy medicine trickled out on to his pink tongue. 'Eeee,' he said, contentedly.

'An early night is called for,' yawned Adam Hope, who had made them all laugh during the meal by relating the various adventures Simon had been having back at Animal Ark. The telephone line had been crackly and faint, but Mr Hope had established that all was going smoothly and happily in their absence.

'Especially as we plan to leave at dawn tomorrow,' Levina reminded them.

'Dawn?' said Paul, sounding a little reluctant.

'The earlier the better,' John Carter agreed. 'I'd like a chance to see Grace again, before I leave. I'll feel better about Jojo's chances if we can at least find her again and work out how quickly we can try to interest her in him.'

Mandy's emotions were mixed as she heard this. She so badly wanted to see Jojo accepted into the family group in the forest, yet she knew that parting from him was going to be very hard.

She picked Jojo up and put him on her hip, smiling at his funny little face. It wouldn't do for Jojo to know what plans were afoot for his future. 'Time for bed,' she told him, and Jojo showed her his gums.

At the first sounds of activity in the camp, Jojo woke Mandy. She opened one eye and gently removed one of his fingers from her ear. Jojo peered intently at the tiny red bites along Mandy's neck, then put his lips to them.

'Not for eating, silly,' she chuckled sleepily. 'I'm the one who's been eaten – fleas, mosquitoes and who knows what other creatures have feasted on me.'

Outside, Levina was stuffing supplies into a series of backpacks. It had been decided to camp near the gorillas that night.

Emily and Adam Hope were sorting through an emergency supply kit and adding items to the first-aid box, while Paul was repacking his cameras. John Carter was singing merrily in the shower hut and Mandy decided to follow him. The water in the oil drum, she judged, squinting up at the tree in which it hung, would be the perfect temperature in the gentle warmth of early morning.

'Bandages, antiseptic creams, insect repellent, camera batteries, binoculars, matches . . .' Emily

Hope was checking off items from a list. 'It's a good thing you are so well-equipped for this job, Levina,' she called.

'Can't take any risks in Africa, Emily,' her friend replied.

Mandy took off Jojo's nappy and sat with him on the grass. He crawled a few paces from her and lay on his tummy, sniffing the ground, then looked round to make sure she was still there.

James came over with a bottle of warm formula milk. 'Shall I feed him?' he asked, shaking the bottle to attract Jojo's attention.

'Yes – I hope he's hungry,' Mandy replied. 'We'll find Grace today, I'm sure we will,' she continued, pleased to see that Jojo was sucking happily at the bottle. 'I'm going to have a shower,' she said, and raced off to get her shampoo and towel. There were some things she simply couldn't do with a gorilla baby on her hip!

After breakfast, they set off into the forest. Smothered in sun cream and insect repellent and wearing a baseball cap, Mandy felt filled with excitement. She carried Jojo, and James, walking behind her, had one of the backpacks strapped to his shoulders. Paul had again asked James to carry one of his cameras and it swung round his neck on a leather strap.

Taking roughly the same route they had taken before, the party trudged through the airless green humidity. When they came to the small river, they rested again, and Manou unwrapped a neat parcel of celery sticks on which he had sprinkled salt. He passed them round, along with the water bottles. The water was warm, but they were all so thirsty, it didn't seem to matter.

Soon after they had started off again, they heard the hollow thumping of leathery paws on a chest. There was a loud simultaneous barking from several gorillas.

Jojo, who had been dozing with his forehead against Mandy's shoulder, was instantly alert and blinking. He shifted round, then half rose on all fours, gripping Mandy's collar with two tightly clenched hands, jigging up and down. It seemed to Mandy as though Jojo was saying, 'Take me to them, please!'

She stroked him soothingly. She was hot and sticky, and the heat from his hairy little body only made her hotter, but she didn't mind a bit.

Levina motioned for them to be quiet, then pointed to her microphone, indicating that she was going to switch it on. Paul's camera began to whirr softly at the same time.

Levina and Paul edged closer, creeping as quietly as possible through the undergrowth to within a few metres of the band of gorillas, at rest in a patch of deep shade.

Following carefully, the others heard her say into the microphone, 'The group have fed – you can see the pile of debris they have left from their foraging. It's too hot for energetic activity; generally a time for grooming . . . a peaceful time of day.'

Mandy noticed that James was watching Paul filming, rather than the gorillas. He seemed fascinated by how the cameraman positioned himself so perfectly and noiselessly for filming, edging ever closer, until it seemed the gorillas could reach out and touch him.

Mandy didn't recognise any of the gorillas they had seen the day before, except for the big, bald-headed male Levina had called Domino. She counted twelve gorillas, in all.

'No sign of Grace, as yet,' John Carter whispered, disappointedly.

The younger gorillas began a game that annoyed the dozing elders. They scooted about on their knuckles, swinging up the lianas and into the lower branches of the trees, then pelted them with twigs and bark ripped up by their claws. Domino gave out a sharp, barking shout of warning.

Jojo chattered softly to himself. Mandy noticed that he seemed less frightened and more interested than he had on their previous visit to the forest. He stood up, with one foot extended on Mandy's hip bone, stretched his neck and called out.

Adam Hope put a finger to his lips. Mandy tried to quieten Jojo by distracting him with her shirt buttons.

And then Mandy heard Levina gasp. Grace had come lumbering slowly into view.

# *Seven*

Grace made her way slowly to a smooth hollow in the trunk of a fig tree and settled herself there. Hearing the noise from Paul's video camera, she looked up intently, staring at the trees, and then down, to look at what she held in the crook of her arm. It lay like a pale streak against Grace's chest, as though somebody had daubed her with a large paintbrush.

Mandy and James realised at the same moment that it was a tiny, newborn gorilla. It lay there, still and quiet, just two round brown eyes staring in bewilderment, above a tiny, grey and crinkled body.

'Probably born a few hours ago,' whispered Levina, as she watched through her binoculars. She passed the binoculars to John Carter.

'Wonderful,' he said softly.

As the others watched silently, Levina moved a little way away, and Mandy could hear the low rumble of her voice as she worked.

When Levina had stopped talking into her microphone, John Carter said, 'I vote we move off for a while and make some plans.'

Levina nodded. 'Back towards the river. We can set up camp there, and still be close enough to make sure Grace becomes as used to our presence in the forest as the rest of the band.'

They retraced their steps to the river, a joyful spring in everyone's step.

But Levina was deep in thought. 'It's a relief to see Grace has stayed around, and given birth,' she said. 'That's two steps nearer for Jojo, of course . . . but she's looking worn out!'

A few paces back from the water's edge, they stamped the vegetation flat beneath a broad, leafy tree with no visible surface roots. The bark of the trunk was crusty with clinging lichen and moss. Above was the low, closed canopy of the forest, hanging like a large umbrella suspended from a cloud.

Kadebe, Paul and Mr Hope began to haul out a ground sheet and a collection of tents that had been rolled up into tiny, waterproof bundles. As the others spread out the picnic that Manou had prepared, the small camp sprang to life and began to look quite homely.

James fetched a pot of water for boiling. 'Scout camp,' he said, 'was never like this. This is the real thing.'

Mandy, who was changing Jojo's nappy, laughed.

'Now,' John Carter began, as they ate lunch, 'sadly, I need to take my leave very soon. But our Grace is now a mother, so let's go over our plan of action.'

'We should get Paul to show us Grace's glade, first of all,' Levina suggested. 'We need to ascertain whether she is still going back there regularly, in order to decide whether it's a suitable place to deposit Jojo.'

'My thoughts, exactly,' John Carter agreed. 'How I wish I could be here longer. I won't rest for a second until I know whether Grace has taken Jojo on. You must promise to telephone me in England the moment you have any news.'

Levina patted his hand. 'Of course. But, you mustn't miss your plane home. When you are ready, I think we should begin the walk back to the main camp. Kadebe will come with us.'

She turned to the others. 'Once we have taken John to his plane, we shall return as quickly as we can. We should be back in about . . .' Levina studied her watch, 'four hours or so? All right?'

'We'll keep a portable radio transmitter here, I presume?' Adam Hope asked.

'Yes,' Levina replied. 'We'll keep in touch. Just allow Grace to be aware of your presence around the area, so that she can begin to realise that you are not threatening her, and start to trust you.'

'I'll carry on filming, Levina,' Paul said. 'I'll get whatever I can. You can edit out the bits you don't want and we can work on the commentary together later, OK?'

'Fine, Paul,' Levina replied. 'I can do the voice-over when I see what you've got.'

Mandy was sad to see John Carter leave. She finished giving Jojo his bottle, squeezed a little ointment on his sore eye and wiped his milky mouth. Then she handed him to Mr Carter for a goodbye cuddle.

Jojo put one arm round Mr Carter's neck and affectionately put a finger in his ear.

'Go well, little friend,' Mr Carter said, looking him in the eye. 'Let's hope Grace gives you the opportunity to grow up here, strong and happy – perhaps even become leader of your band.'

Jojo put his small nose against John Carter's and Mandy's eyes suddenly stung with hot tears. 'We have to succeed, for Mr Carter, as much as for Jojo,' she whispered to James.

James nodded and grinned. 'I hope we will, Mandy.'

As the afternoon sun burned down fiercely on the forest canopy, Mandy grew sticky with the heat and her clothes felt damp. Holding Jojo, who still showed very little interest in leaving her for even a minute, was very like holding a hairy hot-water bottle.

Manou slept with his back against the trunk of a tree. Adam Hope began to doze, his head supported by the sloping bark of a small fig tree. Emily Hope, too, was overcome by the heat, and said she needed to nap. She crawled into one of the tents.

'I'm off to do some more filming,' Paul said. 'And I might look in on Grace's little glade again.'

'We'll come!' Mandy and James spoke at exactly the same time.

'Be careful!' Emily Hope called sleepily from inside the tent.

Jojo clung to Mandy as he slept in her arms. She and James followed Paul back to the gorillas' resting place, picking their way carefully through the tortuous undergrowth and ducking under curly, low-hanging vines.

The gorillas were spread about, resting quietly in the intense afternoon heat. Domino breathed deeply, lying on his back with his knees drawn up. He looked so much like an old man that Mandy and James laughed.

'Shh,' cautioned Paul. 'Hand me that camera, please, James.'

Cha Cha was grooming Kima, whose head was nodding contentedly as she parted the hair on his back, looking for fleas and other tiny, fur-living mites. Mandy recognised an elderly female gorilla Levina had called Zelda. She had a distinctive grey streak on her left side and a shaggy mane of thick hair that almost covered her eyes. Zelda waved her hand above her head to shoo away the flies that buzzed around her, but her eyes were closed. A small distance away from the rest of the band, partially hidden by vegetation, Bruno squatted, watching the others. But Grace was nowhere to be seen.

Mandy felt a stab of disappointment.

James hopped up on to the lower branches of a tree to peer around. 'She must be here somewhere.'

'There!' Paul said. 'There she is.' He began filming.

Grace lumbered into view, looking wearily around her. Her expressive face wore a worried, almost hopeless expression. She held the infant against her side. It appeared to be sleeping, head thrown back and mouth slightly open. It hung there carelessly, looking as though, at any moment, Grace might let it fall. Mandy began to feel fearful for the tiny gorilla.

'She looks frightened . . . or something,' James whispered. 'What's the matter with her?'

'Difficult to be certain,' Paul whispered back. 'I hope she hasn't had a fall-out with Domino.'

Grace paced, breathing hard, and, though

Domino opened one curious eye, he closed it again and dozed on. She looked for a place to sit and, seeing a suitable spot away from the group, she began to walk towards the bush behind which Mandy, James and Paul were crouched.

Grace came nearer, and nearer still, until she was only a couple of metres away from them, then sat down with a deep sigh. She raised her face to sniff the air, as if she knew there were humans close behind her but didn't have the energy to worry about it. Mandy's heart jumped about so hard she was certain Grace would hear it.

And then they saw what they hadn't noticed before: on Grace's back and side were patches where the fur was thinning. Some of the skin showing through looked red and raw. She scratched at herself, raking at her skin so hard it made a loud rasping noise.

'Look!' Mandy whispered urgently, 'some of her hair seems to be falling out – she's all patchy and sore!'

All the while Grace scratched, the infant opened its mouth to search for milk, but Grace did nothing to help it. It whimpered sadly while its mother sat, her nimble fingers seeking to relieve what seemed to be a terrible, all-over itching.

'Poor Grace,' James whispered. 'And poor Jojo – she doesn't look in any state to look after her own baby, let alone another one!'

Paul began packing away his camera equipment. 'Let's get back to camp. We need some veterinary advice on this development,' he said, seriously.

They crept away, and headed back to camp. Mandy's heart was thudding with tension and worry. What if Grace wasn't going to be fit enough to take Jojo before they had to leave for England? They were leaving in only four days!

'I'll walk back with you, then I'll double back and take another look at Grace's hiding-place,' Paul told them, as he led them along the rough path back towards the camp.

When he could see the clearing of tents, he turned to go back into the forest. Mandy, marvelling at Paul's energy, almost ran the last few metres, egged on by a jigging Jojo. He was hungry, Mandy knew, and she felt bad about having gone into the forest without an extra supply of milk for his bottle. His appetite had come back with a vengeance, after the medicine given to them by Dr Umpondo. Now he seemed permanently hungry!

As they arrived back in camp, Adam Hope was stirring something in a large black metal pot that sputtered and splashed on the fire. Manou stood over him, watching, a huge smile on his face.

Emily Hope looked up from cutting carrots into neat slices. 'Successful afternoon?' she asked. 'Where's Paul?'

'He's gone back to look at Grace's private place again,' James told her.

'Grace was there, Mandy said, coming to sit by her mother, 'but she isn't well, Mum. Not well at all!'

Adam Hope looked over, listening to what Mandy was saying.

Mandy explained. 'She came really close up to us and we could see that her skin is all itchy and sore – she keeps scratching and she seems really unhappy and nervous.'

'And she doesn't want to feed her baby,' James added.

Manou took over stirring the pot and Mr Hope walked over. 'Skin looks dry and sore . . .'

he mused. 'Did you get close enough to notice if her coat was falling out?'

'Yes!' Mandy replied. 'She came so close this time we could have almost touched her. Her hair is falling out in patches.'

'Sounds like sarcoptic mange to me,' said Mr Hope. He looked at his wife.

'It sounds exactly like it,' Emily Hope agreed. 'We haven't got the right sort of treatment for mange with us here. But why don't we radio Levina? She can pick up the appropriate treatment at Camp Kahuzi, on her way back here.'

'Good idea,' said Mr Hope. 'Let's give it a try.'

The portable radio transmitter crackled loudly to life. 'Levina?' Adam Hope said. 'Are you there? Come in, please . . .'

There was a noise that sounded to Mandy like waves breaking on a shore . . . then silence.

'Come in, Camp Kahuzi, this is Adam Hope, over . . .'

After several tries, with no reply, Mandy's dad was puzzled. 'Well, that's odd. Not a sign of her.'

'But we have to treat Grace straight away!' Mandy said urgently. 'Otherwise she won't feel well enough to take Jojo on before we have to leave!'

'And what about her own baby?' James added. 'It can't last long without Grace being able to feed it!'

'I know,' Mr Hope said sympathetically. 'But without the right drugs here, I'm afraid there's really nothing we can do. We'll try to get hold of Levina again, soon.'

'And if that doesn't work,' Emily Hope added, 'I'll ask Manou to take me back to the camp, and I'll search through her veterinary drug box myself. How about that?'

'Yes, please, Mum,' Mandy said quietly. She looked down at Jojo. He lay on his back, fiddling with his long black fingers at the sticky tapes on his nappy and making little chattering noises.

Manou came over with a bottle he'd prepared as he listened to what Mandy and James were saying. He offered it to Jojo, who grasped it eagerly and started sucking noisily.

Mandy smiled up at Manou gratefully, then rubbed her eyes and sighed. She was itching all over from the heat and the accumulated dirt of the day, and badly wanted a cool shower and a litre or two of something cold to drink.

'But first of all,' continued Mrs Hope, seeming to read her daughter's mind, 'you two need a wash, a drink and some supper. Manou has boiled up a bucket of river water and it's cooled now for washing.' She lifted Jojo from Mandy, saying, 'This young man will have to put up with me for a while!'

Mandy washed as effectively as she could, splashing cool water from the big iron bucket on the back of her neck and letting it rush down to her feet. It felt good. She changed into a pair of jeans and a long-sleeved T-shirt and pulled on her walking boots. The more skin she covered up, she reasoned, the less there would be for the insects to bite.

'Your turn, James,' she called.

Paul turned up just as Manou was lighting the oil lamps. The little camp looked safe and cosy. A fire roared under the cooking pot, and a delicious savoury smell filled the clearing.

'Aha, what a welcome,' Paul said, collapsing beside Mr Hope. 'I'm beat.'

'Did you find Grace again?' Mandy asked.

'Yep. She'd retreated back to her private little

glade. There are signs that she gave birth there . . .'

'Good,' said Adam Hope. 'Then that's the place we'll take Jojo. But Mandy and James tell us Grace is unwell.'

'Yes,' Paul frowned. 'We got a really good look at her today, up close. She's got a nasty skin condition.'

'From what Mandy and James said, it sounds like mange,' Mrs Hope said.

'Very possibly,' Paul nodded.

'We're trying to get hold of Levina to ask her to bring some medication back for Grace, but we're not having any luck.' Mr Hope picked up the transmitter again. 'Come in, Levina . . .' he said loudly. Again, the radio crackled and buzzed, but there was no reply.

Paul frowned. 'I can't think where she could be. She's had more than enough time to get to the airstrip and back by now . . .'

Time seemed to be passing by very slowly. Mandy hated to think of poor Grace, unable to sleep for the dreadful itching of her skin, her limp, sad little infant whimpering against her.

After Paul had taken his turn at freshening up, Manou dished up dinner. While they were eating, they tried to be cheerful and not worry, but it was difficult.

Paul filled them in a bit more on the background of the local gorilla population. 'The lowland gorillas we have around here were only discovered in 1847,' he began. 'Those that live higher up in the mountain regions are much rarer and were only discovered in 1902. Not long ago, really, is it?'

Adam Hope shook his head. 'The animal most capable of communication with humans,' he mused, 'and yet one of the last to be studied.'

'But they might also be one of the first species to vanish from the planet if we are not careful,' Paul concluded, quietly.

Emily Hope tried to contact Levina again. 'Levina? Can you hear me?' She spoke loudly and clearly into the transmitter.

Nothing.

'Mum,' Mandy began, feeling desperate, 'can't we go and search through Levina's medical box now?'

'No!' Manou spoke up sharply. He had been kneeling over a backpack of provisions. Now he stood up. 'Is too dark now. Is too far – too dangerous. Missy Levina she not come here tonight in dark. She sleepy in town.' He smiled at Mandy. 'Manou and Missus Hope go tomorrow, first thing, OK? No sooner.'

Mandy looked at James. He shrugged his shoulders and smiled in sympathy. She knew that everyone else was concerned about Grace, too. And that Manou was right, of course. She looked down at the sleeping Jojo, then forced herself to smile back. It was going to be a very long night . . .

Manou had built up the fire to ward off nocturnal animals, and the shadows of the flames flickered and jumped on the sides of Mandy's nylon tent. It grew cold and she snuggled deeper into her sleeping bag, Jojo as close to her as he could get, curled up under her chin.

Over the crackle and snap of twigs in the fire, Mandy could hear the distant howls and screams, flutters and coughs of creatures in the forest. She longed for sleep; then the dawn would come more quickly and Manou and her mother could fetch the treatment for Grace. But her last thought, before she finally dropped off, was for Levina. What on earth had become of her?

# Eight

The dawn light that filled Mandy's tent was a misty green colour. Jojo was still fast asleep. She stroked him awake and he lay and blinked at her solemnly, as if trying to remember where he was.

Mandy dressed quickly then picked up Jojo and poked her head into James's tent, next to hers. 'James!' she hissed, 'are you awake?'

'Yeah,' he responded sleepily. 'I heard Manou and your mum leaving,' he mumbled.

'Oh, they've gone already? That's good. Shall we try and make a fire?' Mandy suggested. 'Dad says he's useless until he's had a cup of tea.'

James nodded sleepily and yawned. 'Now we're awake, we might as well be useful,' he said. 'I'll get dressed.'

Mandy went over to the site of last night's fire. All that remained was a big pile of powdery grey ash. The cooking pot had been washed and stood gleaming in the early morning sunlight.

James crawled out of his tent. 'I dreamed of gorillas,' he said. 'Playing football. It was stupid.' He yawned again. 'Let's go and find some twigs and sticks and things.'

They walked a short way into the forest. Mandy began to strip the smaller branches at the bottom of the trees, taking care not to wreck the home of any tiny animal or insect that had made its base there.

Jojo found the task an exciting one and stretched out a small hand, hugging Mandy with his knees, to grasp at leaves. Mandy laughed. 'You're growing up!' she said. 'Good boy, that's right, pull.'

James sifted through the undergrowth, looking for sticks. Suddenly, he pulled up short and gasped.

'Oh, no . . . Mandy!'

Mandy's blood froze at the urgency she heard in her friend's voice. She spun around and leaped over to him. 'What? What is it, James?'

He pointed, his eyes as wide as saucers. Lying among the fallen leaves of the forest floor was Grace's baby. It was curled up on its side, hardly breathing, still and grey-coloured, its eyes closed.

Mandy felt the blood drain from her face. Looking down at the pathetic little body made her eyes fill with hot tears. James was swallowing hard, too.

Quickly, she handed Jojo to James and stooped to lay a hand on the skin of the tiny gorilla. She knew enough by having watched her parents at work to know that if the gorilla's skin was warm, it was a good sign. The baby whimpered when Mandy touched it, and to her relief, there was still some warmth in the tiny body.

Hot tears spilled over and ran freely down her cheeks now. 'I don't know if we should pick it up, James,' she said. 'Perhaps if we do, Grace won't have anything further to do with it.'

They looked around, scrutinising the trees

and the bush beyond. There was no sign of Grace.

'But we can't just walk away, Mandy. It'll die.' James was pale and his glasses had slipped to the end of his nose, but he hadn't bothered to push them back. He gazed down at the baby gorilla, then out at the forest again. 'Pick it up, Mandy,' he said urgently. 'Let's rush it to your dad. He'll know what to do.'

Jojo had twisted away from James in an effort to sniff at the strange little creature on the ground. He jigged and began to chatter noisily.

'Why!' Mandy said, wiping away the tears angrily. 'Why has Grace done this? How could she?' And then a ghastly thought struck her. Maybe Grace had died! What if she wasn't suffering simply from mange? What if it was something even worse; something that had killed her suddenly in the night?

Mandy couldn't bear even to communicate this horrible thought to James. As gently as she could, she lifted the tiny body and held it close to her chest. She hoped the gorilla would feel her heart beating and draw some comfort from it. Its head flopped weakly and it opened its shell-pink mouth and closed it again, hopelessly.

James stroked the baby with trembling hands. 'Come on, let's get back!' he said, urgently.

They abandoned the firewood and ran.

'Mr Hope!' bellowed James as they rushed back into the camp clearing. 'Please, wake up!'

Jojo, entering into the spirit of this new game, shouted, 'Hee, hee, ha!' and stood up on James's hip bone, one hand hooked round the back of his neck.

'Dad!' Mandy shouted, close behind him. 'Dad!'

'Hey, what's all the fuss?' Paul stepped into view, his cameras hanging heavily round his neck, a yellow polishing cloth in his hand.

'It's Grace's baby!' explained James hurriedly. 'We found it in the forest. Grace has dropped it . . . or something,' he continued, trying to wrestle his glasses out of Jojo's hand.

'Are you sure it's Grace's?' Paul asked.

'Dad!' Mandy called again, then nodded at Paul. She just knew it was Grace's baby.

A bleary-eyed Mr Hope stuck his head out of the tent flap, pulling a shirt over his head. 'What is it, love?' he asked urgently. 'Is something wrong?'

'Grace's baby!' Mandy cried. 'Look! We found it on the floor. And Grace was nowhere near it . . .'

Mr Hope examined the skinny bundle in Mandy's arms. 'Oh dear . . .' he said softly. The infant's eyes remained closed. Mr Hope scratched his head. 'The first thing we need to do is get some liquid into the poor little thing,' he said. 'We'll have to try it on some of Jojo's formula milk.'

He turned to Paul. 'Could you make a fire to warm some water, please, Paul? And James, can you fetch some river water in the bucket?'

James and Paul hurried off.

Mr Hope turned back to Mandy. 'Use one of Jojo's blankets and wrap the little thing up, love. It must be kept warm. That will do for a start.'

Once the tiny gorilla was swathed in a blanket, Mr Hope said, 'Now, let's have a proper look.' He fetched a stethoscope from the medical box and listened to the gorilla's heartbeat. 'Heart is beating away steadily,' he said. 'That's good. I don't think it's been on its own for too long. Probably just a little dehydrated and hungry.'

Mandy breathed a sigh of relief.

'And, by the way, make that a she, not an it,' her father smiled.

'Oh,' Mandy said, 'a baby girl! And, hopefully, a sister for Jojo,' she added, quietly.

James staggered back into camp with a bucket brimming with water, and took it over to Paul, who was now getting a fire going.

Mandy took the gorilla over to him. 'It's a girl, James,' she said. 'And Dad thinks she's not too ill.'

'That's great!' James replied. 'Let's have another look at her.'

Paul put the filled kettle onto the fire and came over to look at the infant. 'She's a sweetie,' he said, smiling. 'I guess we'll need to find a name for her, too.'

Mandy looked at James. 'What do you think, James?' she asked. 'You found her.'

James looked down at the tiny scrap huddled in Mandy's arms. 'How about Lily?' he said, a little shyly. 'She looks so pale and delicate . . . She's so tiny we almost crushed her with our feet . . .'

Mandy beamed at him. 'Perfect! She's a little lily of the forest.' She looked at Paul.

'Lily it is, then,' Paul agreed, smiling.

\*   \*   \*

When the bottle was made and the teat screwed on, Jojo reached hungrily for it. 'Oh no,' said James sternly, 'not for you this time, greedy guts.'

Jojo hopped up and down on James's lap, a comical, annoyed expression on his face. He flung out an arm towards Lily, stretching his fingers to reach for her, but James held him back. Jojo blinked up at Mandy and showed her his gums. 'Oooh!' he said, and twiddled his long fingers in Lily's direction.

'Yes, I know,' Mandy said. 'It's all very interesting. But you'll have to wait until she's ready to meet you, Jojo!'

Lily fought the large teat of the bottle, twisting with surprising strength, pushing away from its foreign smell.

Mr Hope instructed Mandy to hold her more firmly, while he opened Lily's tiny mouth with practised fingers to let the warm milk touch her tongue. Then, instinctively, Lily began to suck tentatively at the teat.

As Lily began to suck, Mandy allowed herself to wonder again at what on earth could have happened to Grace that would make her suddenly abandon her baby.

Within a minute or two, Lily was drinking from the bottle as though it was all she had known. A cheer went up from the little group peering anxiously down at her.

Lily opened her eyes and fixed them on James's face. James reached out and stroked Lily's tummy, and she brought up her little black leathery feet and hugged his arm with them.

'Do you want to hold her while she finishes her feed, James?' Mandy offered.

James nodded, and, while Mr Hope took Jojo,

Mandy put the still-sucking Lily into James's arms. Jojo then went to Mandy, with a great neck hug and a 'Hah, hah, ooh!'

James smiled proudly down at Lily, who didn't take her eyes off him. 'That's better, now, isn't it, Lily?' Then the smile left his face and he groaned. 'I think,' he said carefully, 'Lily will have to borrow one of Jojo's . . . um . . . nappies. My trousers are suddenly soaked!'

Everyone laughed, then looked up as Manou, followed by Levina, Mrs Hope and Kadebe, stepped through the bush surround and into the camp.

'Levina!' they chorused. 'You're OK! What happened?'

Levina smilingly held up a hand. 'I'm sorry,' she said. 'I had a little . . . adventure . . . but I can see you have had one of your own!' She stared in amazement at Lily, lying on her back in James's arms, suckling at Jojo's big bottle. 'There's a lot to tell, I can see!'

Relief swept through Mandy and made her legs feel suddenly weak. Levina and her mum were back, and they'd brought the medicine box. Everything might be all right now – if only Grace had survived the night.

# *Nine*

'Mum must have told you,' Mandy started, 'Grace isn't well. And this morning we found she'd left Lily lying on the forest floor and gone off . . . we don't know where!'

Levina frowned. 'Lily?' she asked, then smiled as James pointed at the tiny gorilla that dozed peacefully on his lap. She nodded. 'A lovely choice of name. So we have another female in our band.' She looked at Adam Hope.

'A female,' he confirmed. 'And in perfect health, it seems. Born without apparent signs of difficulty.'

'We found her early this morning,' James

explained. 'Mandy and I had gone a little way into the forest to look for firewood. We were going to surprise Mr Hope and Paul with a cup of tea. I almost stepped on Lily,' he said quietly.

Jojo had crawled over to investigate the small bundle on James's knee. It smelled very interesting and made a snuffly noise as it slept. Jojo held on to Mandy's bootlace with one small hand, and edged along on his bottom until his nose touched the hairless back of the infant. He sniffed, then scampered back to Mandy and jigged his excitement.

Mandy kissed him and offered him a slice of kiwi fruit.

'Are you absolutely sure that Grace was nowhere around, watching over her baby?' Levina asked Mandy.

'Almost certain,' Mandy replied, feeling a little uncomfortable. She looked at James. 'We stood around for a few minutes. There was no noise, no movement . . . no sign of her.'

James nodded. 'But why would she go off like that?' he asked.

'There could be many reasons,' Levina explained. 'It could simply be that she isn't an experienced mother and she didn't know how to care for Lily. Gorillas have to learn the skills of motherhood from their elders, you see.'

Mandy's heart sank. That would mean that Grace wouldn't know how to care for Jojo either.

'Or,' Levina continued, 'it could be that Grace has become too ill to look after Lily . . .'

'That would be my guess,' said Emily Hope, fanning her face with her hat. 'From the sound of it, she is suffering from mange – that's another name for scabies, a nasty parasite that will make her itch and feel pretty awful.'

'Then, what we need to do,' said Levina, 'is treat some fruit with the medication, and get it into Grace as soon as possible.'

'What if she can tell the fruit has been "doctored" and refuses to eat it?' James asked.

'That shouldn't be problem,' Emily Hope replied. 'The drug we have with us is in an oil that doesn't taste bad at all. If we rub it all over the skin of the fruit, we might entice Grace into eating it *and* coming back for more the next day! It's a far kinder way of treating her than putting her to sleep with a drugged dart and taking her into the clinic in a crate.'

'But what if the other gorillas find the fruit

and eat it?' asked James again. 'Will it harm them?'

'No,' Mrs Hope said. 'But the drug will quickly attack Grace's mange and stop the itching immediately – so as soon as we can get some in to her system, the sooner she'll begin to feel better.'

While they got to work, scoring the skins of a large basket of ripe fruit, then carefully oiling them with the scabies medication, Levina explained what had kept her. 'Kadebe and I had said goodbye to John at the airstrip and had left to drive back to Kahuzi. Then, half a mile out of town, the Land-rover stalled and we couldn't get it to start again!'

'Poor Levina,' said Mandy.

'The vehicle was too heavy for us to push, so I decided to walk back into the town to get help. While Kadebe was fiddling with the engine, some children appeared to see what was going on. Kadebe wasn't taking much notice of their chattering so, of course, he didn't see them picking up my radio transmitter and making off with it!'

'Ah,' said Adam Hope. 'No wonder there was silence from your end!'

'I got someone to go out and tow the Land-rover back into town, but we had to stay overnight at Dr Umpondo's house. Then, when we finally made it back to Camp Kahuzi, Emily and Manou were there, collecting medical supplies, with the news that Grace was unwell!'

'Did you get the Land-rover fixed?' Paul asked.

'Yes. It seemed the starter motor had jammed,' Levina said, adding, 'I'm sorry if I worried you all.'

Half an hour later, the fruit was ready.

'I guess the best target for the fruit is Grace's little glade,' Paul suggested, as he packed his camera equipment for the forthcoming trek.

'Good idea,' Emily Hope said. She, Levina and Manou had decided to remain in camp to catch up on their rest, so Paul and Kadebe took up position at the head of the little group, with Mr Hope bringing up the rear.

The mid-morning sun was a blazing orb, and before long Mandy was hot and damp. The crook of her arm, where she supported Jojo, dripped with perspiration.

'I don't know how you've managed to carry Jojo all this time, in this heat,' said James, looking back at her over his shoulder. 'Lily is warm and heavy enough – and she's half his size!' Both Levina and Emily Hope had offered to have Lily that day, but James had said no. He wasn't about to miss this time with Lily, no matter how difficult it got!

Paul led the way expertly to Grace's little glade. A few metres before he reached it, he signalled for the others to crouch down and wait while he went on ahead to inspect the site and see if Grace was there.

Mandy took a moment to rest and look around her. They were not very far from the area where Domino's band usually rested.

Then Paul's head popped up. He waved and made a thumbs-up sign. The others made their way over to what was a bowl-shaped patch of ground, surrounded by a wall of thickly tangled vegetation. In this perfect little glade, Grace had made her own private place. This, Mandy thought, would be a fine place for Jojo to take refuge, should he ever need it.

'Quick, let's unload the fruit!' Paul whispered. 'I'll keep watch for her.'

As Kadebe hauled from his rucksack an oval-shaped, pinkish pawpaw, followed by oranges, apples and figs, James looked over his shoulder nervously, in case Grace came thundering into the glade, furious to find these strange humans in her haven.

'Better make a hasty retreat, now,' Mr Hope said, as soon as Kadebe had finished. 'We don't want to scare her off with our human smell.'

They hurried back into the thick of the forest and began to make their way to the area where the rest of the band tended to congregate, so that Paul could do some more filming.

They found the gorillas sleeping off the heat of midday, as usual. Only Domino strutted about. He seemed tense and alert and frowning. Kima, too, was awake, and his chocolate-coloured eyes were fixed on the leaves rustling gently in the trees above him.

Mandy was relieved to see Bruno still there at the edge of the group, lying on his back in a relaxed posture, dozing. It was clear that, although he was no longer a close member of the family, he had not been chased out either.

Lily seemed unaware that her own kind were grouped just a few metres away. She snuggled in James's arms, like a human baby, wrapped in Jojo's towel, which was now covered with traces of old milk and spilt fruit. Jojo began to hoot happily, calling across to the creatures he recognised as his own.

'Shh!' Mandy told him urgently. Jojo looked at her and pressed his face into her shirt.

Domino turned slowly and stared over in their direction. With a sideways glance, he began a hesitant walk towards them, sniffing deeply at the air. This time, Mandy thought her heart would stop beating altogether. She covered Jojo's eyes, praying he would not call out to the huge gorilla as he approached.

But Domino was suddenly distracted by a slight movement to his right. In the deep shade of the forest canopy, Grace was standing, quite still, looking longingly at the group from some distance away. She took a step forward, cautiously, and looked at Domino, challenging him for permission to enter.

Paul's camera whirred into action.

James groaned in dismay. 'Oh, look at the state of her!'

Even from where they stood, several metres away, they could see the dullness of Grace's coat and her skin showing through in several large, bald patches. Scabs had formed where she had rubbed the skin raw. She scratched insistently, first this side, then that.

Domino scrutinised her, summing her up. And then he opened his enormous mouth and let out a deafening, barking scream. He banged loudly on his big chest then scooted at Grace in a full, angry gallop. Sensing that he meant business, poor Grace turned and fled, rushing noisily through the bushes to be swallowed up again by the dense greenery.

Mandy, like the others, stood rooted to the spot, shocked to the core. But Paul's camera still whirred away quietly for a while, until

Domino, satisfied that she had left, stopped and wandered back to his band.

'What was all that about?' James whispered urgently.

Paul shook his head. 'I would guess that Domino decided that Grace, being so obviously ill, might put the rest of his band at risk,' he replied. 'He doesn't want her around any more.'

Feeling a hopeless sense of failure and sadness, Mandy followed the subdued party back to the temporary camp. What chance would they have now of getting Grace to care for Lily and Jojo? She might have been frightened away for good. And if she was too scared to return to her own little glade nearby, she wouldn't get better, either. The medicated fruit would just sit there and rot. It was too much to bear.

Back at the temporary camp, they related the events to Levina and Emily Hope.

'Well, that's a blow,' said Levina sadly. 'We might just have succeeded if things had gone smoothly. If Grace had eaten the fruit today, then she might have felt well enough for us to offer Jojo and Lily to her just before you are due to leave. But – after Domino's reaction to Grace this morning – it's unlikely she'll return straight away, if at all . . .'

Manou offered a belated breakfast, but no one had any appetite. They sat around sipping tea, each of them lost in their own thoughts.

'We'll just have to go back to Camp Kahuzi,' Levina concluded, quietly.

'But what if Grace *does* decide to go back to her own little glade today, and eat the fruit?' Mandy cried. 'She just might, and then we could still be in with a chance!' She looked at the faces around her. 'Let's wait and see – just one more day!' she pleaded.

Levina looked across at Emily and Adam Hope, then back at Mandy's pleading face. 'Well . . .' she said, 'we do have enough supplies—'

'Oh, thanks, Levina!' Mandy said, jumping up and giving her a hug.

'We'll go to Grace's glade one more time, then, and wait a while to see if she turns up.'

'Goodness, we're going to be as fit as gladiators on our return home!' Emily Hope laughed. 'But, yes, I'm game.'

'Well, then,' said Adam Hope, 'what are we waiting for?'

\* \* \*

A light, misty rain began to fall as they made their way back to Grace's glade. Once again, Paul took charge and went on ahead to peer about for signs that Grace had been there. The others hung back, waiting and hoping for good news.

But when Paul next appeared, he was frowning. Mandy's heart sank. She looked at James, who, hugging Lily to him, shrugged back disappointedly.

Paul picked his way quietly over and around the thick tangle of bush to where the others waited. 'Difficult to tell,' he concluded. 'Some of the fruit has gone, but Grace might have taken that *before* her run-in with Domino. There's no sign that she's been here very recently.'

'Well, at least she'll be feeling a bit better,' James said.

'And she *might* have come and eaten the fruit after Domino roared at her – which means she won't be too scared to come here again!' Mandy added, determinedly.

Levina smiled. 'We might as well look on the bright side,' she agreed. 'So I suggest we make ourselves comfortable, and wait to see if Grace turns up.'

They settled down, prepared to wait as long as they needed for Grace to make an appearance.

James fed Lily, while Mandy amused Jojo by picking bits of bark off a tree. He soon got the hang of it and took great delight in the game.

The rest of the day passed slowly, with no sign of Grace. As the sun began to set, the creatures in the forest began to make preparations for the coming night; the bird call began to quieten and the night crickets began to shrill. Mandy hoped desperately that Grace would return to her private haven to sleep.

The light began to fade, and still there was no sign of Grace. Mandy knew that time was finally running out.

Eventually, Levina said the dreaded words: 'I'm afraid we have done all that we can. It's time to leave.'

# Ten

Little was said during the trek back into Camp Kahuzi the following morning. Walking along behind her mother, with Jojo riding merrily on her back, Mandy remembered they hadn't had any breakfast. Nobody had seemed to want to eat, and Kadebe and Manou had packed up the little 'kitchen' without suggesting it. Mandy felt as if a great weight pressed on her heart.

'Look, Mandy!' said Mr Hope, pointing to the sky. 'A crowned eagle! Isn't it magnificent?' Mandy saw the broad, short wings of the huge bird swoop and dive low over the trees, its long tail spread out behind like the tail of a kite. She smiled at her father. She knew he was trying to cheer her up.

The first thing they saw when they arrived at Camp Kahuzi was that James's tent had been flattened. 'Rumba's been visiting!' groaned James and hurried forward to inspect the damage, waking a sleeping Lily. 'No harm's been done,' he called to the others, 'but he's been nosing about again.'

Manou disappeared into the kitchen and began to prepare a meal.

'I'll have a shower, if nobody else wants one first,' Mandy said. She deposited Jojo in his nursery, then collected her soap case, shampoo and towel, before stepping round the canvas curtain to brave what promised to be scalding water.

The cubicle was filled with the crawling bodies of a hundred species of insects, plus a couple of sleepy geckos and a lizard or two. She drew back the curtain, clapped her hands and they wriggled and flew away.

A change of clothes was a great relief and, when she was dressed, Mandy went to find James.

'I'm just on my way to the kitchen to get some milk for Lily,' he said.

Mandy walked over with him. But, as James put out a hand to pull open the flyscreen of the kitchen, he stopped, put a finger to his lips, then indicated to Mandy to listen. Voices were coming from within.

'I have to go into town later for supplies,' Levina was saying. 'I'll telephone John Carter while I'm there. He'll have to make arrangements for the zoo to take Jojo back – and take Lily on too.'

'What a shame,' came Adam Hope's voice. 'John will be bitterly disappointed.'

'It's going to break Mandy's heart,' said Mrs Hope. 'And James's.'

'I know,' said Levina sadly, 'but we've done all we can. Grace was our only chance here. And now that chance has gone.'

Mandy looked at James in horror. She had a sudden, clear vision of Jojo and Lily being put into a wooden crate and loaded on to a plane.

The adults stopped talking as soon as they saw Mandy and James come in.

'Hello, you two,' smiled Mrs Hope. 'Feeding time, is it?'

'Yep,' said Mandy, kissing Jojo's ear. 'It's that time again.' She was trying to be cheerful.

Manou had cooked a great pot of rice and vegetables as a kind of brunch. There was plenty of it, as he hadn't had time to bake bread.

'Levina's going into town, later,' Mr Hope said. 'Why don't we all go with her? Do some shopping for presents before we leave tomorrow?'

Mandy knew her dad was trying to take her and James's mind off their troubles.

'Good idea,' said Emily Hope. 'We can browse around that little craft market we noticed last time we were in town, and find gifts for Simon and Jean, and Gran and Grandad.' She looked at Mandy and James. 'How about it?' she said encouragingly.

Mandy and James said they'd prefer to stay around the camp with Jojo and Lily, if nobody minded.

Mandy knew that James was feeling the same way as her. They would rather spend every moment they could with Jojo and Lily, here in the jungle.

Mrs Hope sighed. 'I don't see why not,' she said, if you really want to.'

'Well, I'll be around,' Paul said. 'I'm going to take some time out to give my camera equipment a good clean, ready for the next development – sad though it will be,' he finished quietly. Everyone knew he was talking about flying Jojo and Lily back to England.

Levina stood up. 'We'd better get going – Adam, Emily?' She turned to Mandy and James. 'Take care, you two. We'll see you later.'

As soon as the Land-rover had been waved off, Paul went to his tent and got on with sorting out his camera equipment.

Mandy still stood there, staring ahead, even though the Land-rover had disappeared from view.

'You seem to be thinking hard,' James joked, half-heartedly.

'I am,' Mandy replied. She turned to him. 'Why don't we?' she said, seriously.

'Why don't we what?' said James.

'Go back to Grace's glade,' Mandy replied. 'Have one more try. If we don't, I'll always wonder whether Grace might have returned to her secret place, feeling better after taking the scabies medication, and wanting her baby back . . .?

James looked at Mandy, mulling the idea over. 'We'd have to persuade Paul to take us,' he said slowly. 'He knows the way, and would know what to do if things get dangerous.'

Mandy nodded. 'I'm sure we could persuade him. Imagine what fantastic filming he could do, if we succeed!'

'OK,' said James. 'You're on. I mean, we're on. Let's go and see Paul.'

'I thought it was going to be much harder to convince him to take us,' James whispered, as Paul led them back towards the towering jungle canopy, half an hour later. 'I thought he would say it was too dangerous or something.'

Once more, rucksacks were packed up with a first-aid kit, a water bottle, some fruit, spare nappies, and two bottles of formula milk for Jojo and Lily.

Mandy was tired; her calf muscles were on fire from all the walking she'd been doing and she had a blister on her heel, but her heart fluttered with excitement. 'Jojo seems to know we're going back into the forest where the gorillas are,' she said, tickling his chest. 'His eyes are darting around like a little child in a sweet shop!'

'Or a big child,' James teased. 'Mrs McFarlane would go out of business if you stopped buying your sweets there!' Mrs McFarlane ran the village post office back home in Welford, where she also had an extensive selection of confectionery.

Mandy pretended to look outraged, then laughed as James tripped over a tree root.

James looked down at Lily, then smiled. His stumble hadn't woken her up. She slept on, wrapped in the old towel in his arms, the pale fur of her tiny head sticking up like a halo round her face.

They passed a cluster of sleeping nests that had been made by the gorillas the night before. The circles of trampled twigs and leaves looked so comfortable, Mandy thought she might like to sleep in one herself. But a powerful smell rose up from them, and flies hummed and buzzed above them, so they hurried past.

At last, Paul came to a halt. Mandy recognised the now-familiar screen of vegetation that surrounded the little glade Grace had made her own.

Paul held up a hand to shield his eyes from the glare and looked long and hard, scrutinising the surrounding area carefully for a sign of Grace. Then, signalling Mandy and James to remain where they were, he made his way over to look down into the sheltered glade.

He soon returned, shaking his head. 'Not there,' he said. 'But the good news is, she could have been back, as more of the fruit has gone.'

They sat down to wait. Jojo lay sprawled on his tummy across Mandy's knees, his chin on her leg. Suddenly, he gave a violent jerk. Mandy looked down to see a column of large black ants marching purposefully through the undergrowth. Jojo pulled himself upright and jigged excitedly.

'Ants,' Mandy told him, 'only ants, silly.'

Jojo was fascinated. He tried to grab the hurrying insects, making chattering noises. 'Hoo, hah!' he said, and reached down to see what the creatures might taste like. A large ant crawled on to Jojo's hand and bit him. Jojo let out a shriek of protest and scurried up and under Mandy's chin, chattering to himself.

'We'd better move,' said Paul, eyeing the ants. 'These biting ants are ferocious.'

James stood up. 'Ugh, yes, let's move—' he began, then he whispered urgently: 'Oh, look!'

Mandy was kissing the palm of Jojo's sore hand but she looked up quickly. Ten metres away, sitting as still as stone, was Grace. She had appeared as if by magic, creeping tentatively out of cover to investigate the sounds and the scent of the visitors.

Paul had automatically reached for his camera. 'She must have been nearby for a while,' he said, quietly. 'She must have heard Jojo shrieking. Probably brought out her maternal instincts.'

Grace lifted her head and sniffed deeply at the air. She looked directly at them, cocking her head as if in puzzlement.

'She can smell her baby and Jojo,' Paul smiled.

Mandy realised she had been holding her breath so long she had to expel it in a rush. James was gripping on to Mandy's T-shirt so hard she thought he might rip the fabric. She shrugged him off. 'What do we do now?' she said, breathless with nerves and excitement.

'Just wait a while,' Paul said. 'Let's see

what she's going to do next.'

'She's not scratching,' James whispered. 'Not at all, see?'

Grace seemed calm and untroubled by her skin complaint, though even from the distance they were Mandy was able to see several large, bare patches in her coat. She sat for several minutes, then rose and moved off again, vanishing into the bush on the other side of the glade.

'Oh, Grace,' whispered Mandy. 'Don't go away again, please!'

'Hang on, Mandy,' said Paul. 'This might be just what we need.'

'What do you mean?' she asked, surprised.

'A chance to put Jojo and Lily into Grace's glade, when we know she's not too far away.'

Mandy sucked in a breath. 'You mean, leave them there? Now?'

James looked at Paul, who nodded at him. 'This is going to be our only chance, Mandy,' he said. 'It has to be now.'

Mandy looked down at Jojo, who seemed to sense the tension in the air and jigged up and down on her hip, burying his face into her neck.

She nodded, then began to remove Jojo's bulky white nappy.

James took off Lily's, so big on her that it came up under her armpits, then put both nappies into a bag, to dispose of back at camp.

'Ready?' Paul said.

Mandy and James looked at each other, then nodded.

They followed Paul around the semi-circle of bush that enclosed Grace's glade. Mandy stooped to enter with a pounding heart. What if Grace was hiding somewhere Paul hadn't noticed in the dense bushes nearby and came charging at them?

First James lay Lily down gently on the grass that had been trampled smooth and flat. She turned her head and mewled, her tiny hands curling and uncurling, looking for something to cling on to.

Then Mandy put Jojo down beside her. Lily crawled close to him and put her arms round his chest. Jojo didn't seem to mind. He looped an arm round her neck and looked about him.

'Shall we say goodbye?' James whispered shakily. 'Just in case . . .?'

Mandy's eyes stung with tears. She nodded.

James took off his glasses and bent to stroke the tiny gorillas.

Mandy looked into Jojo's chocolate eyes. 'You'll be fine,' she told him. She kissed his little face and stroked his ears. 'I've loved being your mum. Let's hope Grace will take care of you now.'

'Bye, Lily,' James said, then couldn't seem to stop himself from adding, 'Don't worry. If your mum doesn't come, we'll fetch you back.'

There didn't seem anything else to say. They backed away, their eyes on the two little gorillas lying in each other's arms on the grass in the sun.

They followed Paul silently out of the glade and found a place to wait where the infants were still visible. Mandy wiped away a trickling tear as they settled down to watch.

The sound of Jojo softly chattering came clearly from within the glade. Mandy could see him grooming Lily, parting the sparse hair on her tiny body with his fingers. Lily was calm, gazing up at Jojo with wide eyes. It was a peaceful scene and Mandy felt happy and sad all at once.

'We're close enough to rescue them if—' James began, then stopped. A gorilla had come into view.

But it wasn't Grace. It was a male, with a tuft of ginger-coloured hair on the top of its massive head. The gorilla raised his face and sniffed at the air – then walked in the direction of the little glade.

Mandy felt a wave of fear flood through her. 'Oh, James, what have we done?' she whispered, terrified. 'What if he harms the babies?'

James had gone pale. He covered his mouth with both hands. He looked ready to spring into the glade and snatch Lily and Jojo to safety – but Mandy knew he couldn't do so without endangering his own life.

The gorilla blinked steadily at the sight of the two infants. He walked in a circle, slowly, around the two small bodies on the ground, examining his strange discovery.

'It's Bruno,' Paul said. 'Remember, the loser in the fight for dominance we saw a few days ago?'

Mandy and James nodded, not taking their eyes from what was happening in Grace's glade. This time it was Mandy's turn to grip on to

James's T-shirt. But James didn't seem to even to notice.

Bruno yawned and scratched his chest. Then Grace came into view.

'Grace!' Mandy whispered. 'Oh, Grace, you've come. Thank heavens!'

As Grace entered the glade, Bruno got up and ambled to meet her. He pressed his forehead up against hers, a sign of partnership and trust.

Grace briefly acknowledged Bruno, but had eyes only for the two gorilla infants on the ground.

Jojo had begun chattering and jigging about, turning circles of excitement on his bottom.

Grace sat down next to Lily and Jojo. Occasionally she scratched herself, but it wasn't the frantic and anguished scratching of the previous day. She began rocking herself from side to side, making a small crooning noise.

Lily wailed loudly and Jojo put a brotherly arm round her. 'Hee!' Jojo said to Grace. 'Ha! Ha!'

Suddenly, Grace put out a huge, hairy arm and scooped Lily up against her chest. Lily instantly searched for her mother's milk, and soon found it.

Having settled Lily, Grace put out a hand to Jojo. Gratefully, the small gorilla shuffled on his bottom towards her, then collided with her big, warm tummy and hid his head there.

Grace sniffed at him, then put her hand on his small head. She gave a big sigh, then looked proudly across to Bruno. 'See?' she seemed to be saying. 'You and I have got a ready-made family. Aren't we lucky?'

'Well, well, well . . .' Mandy and James jumped in unison. They had been so transfixed they'd virtually forgotten Paul was there, quietly capturing the whole thing on videotape. He continued to stand there, filming every second. 'Never seen anything like it . . .' he said, in awe. 'Got it all on tape.'

Mandy was almost choking with relief and pride. 'We've done it, James. It worked!' She realised she was still clutching his T-shirt, and quickly let go, trying to pat out the scrunched-up creases.

'Leave it, Mandy, who cares!' James said, trying to laugh quietly. 'Grace has a family of her own now – and by the look of things, a new mate!'

'Yes,' chuckled Paul. 'Good old Bruno. Grace

doesn't need to worry about being cast out of Domino's band now. She's got Bruno to protect her and her family.'

'What will they do now?' Mandy asked.

'Bruno will most likely take Grace and the family off to another part of the forest and a start a new band of his own,' Paul replied.

For a long time, Mandy, James and Paul sat watching the new family in the glade. The sky was changing to the colours of early evening, but no one could bring themselves to leave, knowing that what they were watching was a once-in-a-lifetime experience.

As the sun began to sink, Paul said it was time for them to go back to Camp Kahuzi, as the others would be back, and beginning to worry.

Reluctantly, Mandy and James agreed.

Mandy, James and Paul arrived back at Camp Kahuzi, bursting with excitement about what had just happened. Levina and Mr and Mrs Hope had returned from town a while earlier, and were worriedly preparing to set out, with Kadabe and Manou, on a dangerous night trek to search for the missing party.

'Where on *earth* have you been?' Mrs Hope called out, as soon as Mandy and James came into view, the worry clear in her voice.

'Sorry, Mum – sorry, Dad!' Mandy called back, 'but we're all OK – and before you tell us off, we've got something to tell you!'

Driving away from Camp Kahuzi, en route to the airport the next day, Levina surprised them all by pulling up at a sleek, white airport hotel. She parked the camp truck under the shade of a fringed canopy. Already parked under the canopy was the camp Land-rover.

'Oh,' James guessed, 'is Paul here?' The cameraman had said he had an appointment in town, but would come along later, to say goodbye at the airstrip.

Levina nodded, smiling.

'Are we going in for a farewell drink?' Emily Hope asked. 'We are rather early for the first leg of our flight home.'

'Well . . .' said Levina cryptically, 'there will be drinks available . . . but, hopefully, we'll have something much more special than that for you!'

Mandy and James looked at each other,

intrigued. They looked at Adam and Emily Hope, who shook their heads.

Levina laughed. 'Paul has brought the video-tape footage he's filmed so far, and should, at this very moment, be setting it up to be shown here at the hotel. The owner of the hotel is a good friend and sponsor of Camp Kahuzi,' she explained. 'We thought you'd like to see it – and I certainly want to see Grace gathering up her new family!'

Mandy gasped. 'Oh, how fantastic, Levina!' A chance to see Jojo again, before she left – even if only on video – was more than she had hoped for. She smiled at James. 'And you'll see Lily too!'

James grinned. 'Good old Lily. Good little Lily, I mean—'

'Wonderful!' said Mr Hope. 'I'd welcome a chance to see if Grace's mange has cleared up as we hoped,' he said, looking at his wife. Emily Hope smiled back.

'Well, it seems she has been taking the fruit with the drugs in it very willingly, as you know,' Levina replied. 'And we'll keep on dosing her until she seems completely clear of the infestation.'

'It seems as though we have a true success story on our hands,' Mrs Hope said. 'But, good heavens, what on earth would I have said to James's parents had anything gone wrong!' She looked sternly at Mandy and James, then her face softened again. 'But, as it turned out, you were able to do a wonderful thing.'

Mandy gave her mum a hug.

'We trusted Paul to look after us,' James put in. 'We wouldn't have done it if Paul hadn't agreed to go with us, would we, Mandy?'

'Er . . .' Mandy wasn't sure about that one, when it came down to it . . .

'Anyway, they didn't come to any harm, that's the important thing.' Mr Hope took over, getting Mandy out of the awkward moment of truth. 'And we're all pretty proud of you both!'

They clambered out of the truck and followed Levina into the air-conditioned lobby of the hotel. A man in a smart white suit came over to greet Levina. Mandy couldn't help thinking how Jojo would have loved the shiny gold buttons on his jacket.

'This is Mr Finch, the hotel manager,' Levina told them. 'These are my friends from England.'

Mr Finch bowed politely from his very large waist and one shiny gold button popped off his jacket and rolled silently across the carpet. Mandy stifled a giggle and dug James in the ribs with her elbow. She saw he was trying hard not to laugh.

'Welcome,' Mr Finch said. 'Mr Wilkie is just about ready for you. If you would like to follow me . . .'

They walked behind the manager to a windowless room with a large white cinema screen against one wall. A collection of straight-backed chairs were arranged in a semicircle.

Levina gestured for them all to take a seat. Mandy looked around for Paul.

'Over there, see?' Levina was pointing to the back of the room, where Paul was bent over a video machine.

The lights dimmed slowly, then the room was suddenly quite dark. Up on the screen was Domino, frowning intelligently as he carefully examined the tangled contents of a night nest. There was juice from a ripe fig on his chin and Mandy was surprised how close up he appeared through the powerful lens of Paul's camera.

'I'm glad we weren't actually that close,' James whispered to Mandy.

Paul's film, narrated in parts by Levina's calm, soft voice, brought vividly to life some of the special moments of their time in the Kahuzi National Park.

When Jojo first appeared on screen, Mandy didn't know whether she wanted to laugh or cry. There he was, blinking his big, round eyes slowly at the strange faces looking in on him, clutching at John Carter's familiar neck and hiding his frightened little face.

There were shots of Jojo drinking his milk, the bottle held between his feet; Jojo lifting his lips in glee and Jojo circling happily in the dirt on his big, white nappy. Mandy was lost in wonderful memories of him.

'Look!' James said urgently. 'There she is. There's Lily . . .'

The film rolled on, charting the adventure of the last few days, and ending up with yesterday's footage. The camera zoomed in on Grace's glade.

As the film drew towards its end, Bruno, sat there, yawning and scratching slowly. But his eyes darted this way and that, proud and alert, watching over the little family he had so recently made his own.

Grace sat hunched protectively over Lily and Jojo. The haunted, weary look had gone from her eyes. She was getting well again.

Jojo seized Lily's tiny foot and was having a game with her toes, while Lily clutched at her mother's arm, a handful of her fur in one small fist, as though she would never let go.

Finally, the camera moved on up into the leaves of the tree and upwards still, to focus on a sky streaked red and gold by a setting sun.

When the lights came on in the room, Mandy struggled for a second to remember where she was. She looked blankly at James.

James grinned, took off his glasses and rubbed his eyes, then put them back on again. 'Um . . . airport hotel. Soon to fly home . . . to England. Remember? Back to school . . . Animal Ark and all that?'

'Yes,' said Mandy. 'I remember. But . . . wasn't it a fantastic holiday, James?'

'The best,' he said, as they stood up to go.

# ANIMAL
## ACTION

If you like *Animal Ark* then you'll love the RSPCA's Animal Action Club! Anyone aged 13 or under can become a member for just £5.50 a year. Join up and you can look forward to six issues of Animal Action magazine - each one is bursting with animal news, competitions, features, posters and celebrity interviews. Plus we'll send you a fantastic joining pack too!

**To be really animal-friendly just complete the form – a photocopy is fine – and send it, with a cheque or postal order for £5.50**

**(made payable to the RSPCA), to Animal Action Club, RSPCA, Causeway, Horsham, West Sussex RH12 1HG. We'll then send you a joining pack and your first copy of *Animal Action*.**

Registered charity no 219099

# Don't delay, join today!

**Name**
.................................................................

**Address**
.................................................................

.................................................................

................................................... **Postcode**
.................................................................

**Date of birth**
.................................................................

Youth membership of the Royal Society for the Prevention of Cruelty to Animals

AACHOD2